THE BOY ASKS AND THE LAKE REPLIED

George Goodwin

iUniverse, Inc.
New York Bloomington

iUniverse books may be ordered through booksellers or by contacting:

iUniverse
1663 Liberty Drive
Bloomington, IN 47403
www.iuniverse.com
1-800-Authors (1-800-288-4677)

Because of the dynamic nature of the Internet, any Web addresses or links contained in this book may have changed since publication and may no longer be valid. The views expressed in this work are solely those of the author and do not necessarily reflect the views of the publisher, and the publisher hereby disclaims any responsibility for them.

ISBN: 978-1-4401-6460-6 (sc)
ISBN: 978-1-4401-6461-3 (dj)
ISBN: 978-1-4401-6519-1 (ebook)

Printed in the United States of America

iUniverse rev. date: 09/22/09

Contents

THE BOY ASKS AND THE LAKE REPLIED

The story is about a man from the North who integrated a town in North Carolina under the guise of remodeling the house on an old tobacco plantation, and changed a nine year old colored ragamuffin into a State Senator.

CHAPTER 1

THE BEGINNING

I first met Bay Lee when I bought a house to remodel. The house had been the main house on a large tobacco plantation in North Carolina and was in horrible shape. I bought a trailer to live in while I remodeled the house. The first day on the job, I had stopped for lunch. I didn't have any electricity, so was having peanut butter and jelly sandwiches and milk to drink. My first visitor was like an apparition. A young kid about nine years old, filthy dirty, long hair, ragged clothes and I thought to myself, this kid has no parents.

I asked him if he had lunch and he said "no". So I made him a peanut butter and jelly sandwich. Evidently he hadn't eaten for days. He jammed the whole sandwich in his mouth, without chewing. I asked if he would like another sandwich and he said "yes". I made him another and told him he had to eat this one slowly and take time to chew it. He then asked if he could have two sandwiches for his brother and sister. I said, "Why don't you go get your brother and sister. They may want more than one sandwich." The kid went next door to a house almost as bad as mine and shortly came out with his brother and sister who were younger than he. They were just as dirty and unkempt as he was also as hungry. They finished the bread and the milk.

But I am way ahead of my story. Let me begin at the beginning. Although the story centers about Bay Lee, I must tell you how I got there.

CHAPTER 2

LUCY

I met my wife, Lucy, when we were in high school. We were sweethearts from the time we first met, although we didn't get married until we graduated from college. We were always very close and never dated anyone else. Our relations were always platonic, even though we did everything together. Our families always expected us to get married.

My father had a home construction company and I had always worked for him during my spare time. My college curriculum was design and business aspects of running this business so we could expand. Since my father had always been successful, this was easy, when I joined the company full time.

After graduation from college, Lucy and I were planning our wedding. We bought a small house and Lucy spent her time furnishing and decorating the house. Finally the big day arrived. We were married in the church and all our friends and family were there. The first part of our dreams was finally coming true.

Since we were very busy in the business of building houses, we planned just a few days for the honeymoon. We would go to New

York City, see the sights, eat at some famous restaurants, see a couple of shows and get acquainted with married life. We saw the Statue of Liberty, viewed New York City from atop the Empire State Building. We went to Mama Leone's for a good spaghetti dinner and had Chinese food in Chinatown. The thing that impressed us most was how busy everyone was, and how much of a hurry everyone appeared to be. I don't remember the names of the shows because we didn't really enjoy them that much. Although we enjoyed the trip, it was a relief to be on the plane for the trip back home and to get settled into family life.

Lucy applied for and got a substitute teaching job at the local grammar school. She had majored in this in college, but didn't want to be tied down to a full time job. The construction business was doing well, so finances were not important. We quickly settled into married life, and doing things with family and friends.

We had always planned to have three children. After about a year, Lucy told me she thought she was pregnant, so we selected a good doctor. The pregnancy went without any problems, with of course, the worry that everything wouldn't be all right. We had a sonogram to be sure and to verify the sex of the child. The first child would be a girl, and we decided to call her Emily, which had been her great grandmother's name. All the grandparents were ecstatic and could hardly wait until she was born. In the meantime we were swamped with baby furniture and clothes. Our friends had a baby shower and we received more baby clothes and diapers. I thought we would have enough diapers for six babies. Little did I know, we ran out in a couple of months.

Emily was a wonderful baby, good disposition, slept all night long, most nights and was never sick, except an occasional colic. We spoiled her terribly and both grandparents were even worse. We now knew what it was like to be a family. Lucy quit her job so she could stay home and take care of Emily.

When Emily was two, Lucy told me she thought she was pregnant again. Since Emily was still seeing the same doctor, Lucy had no trouble getting an appointment and we started the same process again.

Lucy had more trouble with this pregnancy, more morning sickness and sleepless nights. Finally the sonogram. This one was to be a boy and everything appeared to be all right, but Lucy continued with morning sickness and aches in her back. She gained more weight this time and was generally more uncomfortable. We decided we would need more room in the house, so we decided to add two more rooms and a bath to the house. This was not a problem, as I just diverted a crew and in a short time it was completed. Emily still slept in the crib, so we had to buy her a bed and dresser. Emily was walking and talking quite well and used to pat Lucy's belly and say "Baby". We decided to call him Dan. In due time, Dan was born. There was not as much excitement this time. Lucy was happy to have this pregnancy over as she had had so much discomfort. When we got Dan home, he was far different than Emily. He always seemed to have colic and almost always woke up at night and cried. Even though he got the same treatment as Emily, he always seemed to be uncomfortable. Having the children brought Lucy and I even closer. We still did everything together and really enjoyed our life together.

When Dan was about a year and a half old, my father complained of not feeling well. The family doctor's diagnosis was a slight stroke, so he was sent to a cardiologist for testing. The tests confirmed heart problems, and the doctor ordered operations to repair leaky valves. The operations were a success, but Dad never returned to work full time. We arranged a financial settlement, so Dad and Mom would never have to worry about money. This left me in complete charge of the business and it continued to be successful.

In the meantime Lucy became pregnant again. This one turned

to be more like the first pregnancy, not so much morning sickness, sleepless nights or back aches. Dan had finally got over his colic and could sleep all night. And finally came the sonogram, another girl, we decided to call her Sarah.

Emily had started pre-school, so we became active in school activities. As soon as Sarah was born, it became evident that we had three different personalities, Emily was reserved, Dan was studious, and Sarah was always laughing. We realized that with three growing children, we really needed a bigger house. We selected a site in the suburbs and built a new house, taking into account what the kids would need to play, both inside and out, as they grew up and had friends visiting. It seems like only yesterday that we moved into the new house, but the kids are all in school. We go to school meetings, little league, dance recitals and all the other activities of kids in school. Lucy has taught the kids how to study, so they are all good students. Both Emily and Dan always study and have excellent grades, but Sarah is laughing and is light hearted and really doesn't care about her grades. Lucy has her hands full, driving the kids to all their appointments, and I keep busy with the business. It has its ups and downs, but is still very successful. Finances have never been a factor in our lives. Lucy and I still spend a lot of time together and we depend on each other. The next few years pass very quickly.

Emily is a senior in high school; she is planning on going to college and wants to be a teacher. Dan is a sophomore and wants to go into pre-med. We have always planned on the kids going to college. Both Emily and Dan have high grade averages and may get scholarships. But Sarah is another story. She laughs her way through life; her grades are usually C's with an occasional B. About this time, Lucy's father develops cancer. It develops rapidly and within a year he is gone. My parents have been spending winters in Florida, and they decide to move there year round. Both Lucy and I are still busy with school activities. We are so proud of Emily. She is valedictorian of her class and has received a scholarship to college that will pay much of her expenses. Before we realize it, Dan is graduating high school. He is also valedictorian and gets a small scholarship that will help with his pre-med. While all this is happening, Sarah is still laughing her way through grade school.

By the time she is in tenth grade, she suddenly develops an interest in the building industry. She is interested both kitchen and bathroom design. She is constantly pouring over literature and wants to attend all the trade shows to meet the designers and manufacturers to see if they will build what she wants. Usually she calls Mr. Childs, whose factory is in a large city about one hundred miles away. When the innovation was made, it became an item she could always order. Sarah had become a wonderful addition to our company and people would choose our company just to get her designs. Sarah had built a wonderful reputation. About a week before Sarah's graduation, I got a phone call from Mr. Childs. Could we have lunch? Since Sarah had always handled the business with Mr. Childs, I wondered what this could be about. A bomb shell was about to drop. He suggested that we meet at a very nice restaurant and I bring Lucy and Sarah with me. He would make the arrangements. We arrived at the restaurant and Mr. Childs was waiting for us. He had brought Mrs. Childs and his son Derrick with him. Derrick was a couple of years older than Sarah and was in college, and worked part time. I had met Derrick before. He had been in charge of the installations of the fancy kitchens, but I did not know he was Mr. Childs' son. The seating arrangement was simple. I sat next to Mr. Childs and Sarah sat next to Derrick. Sarah had never had much interest in boys and it soon became obvious why.

Sarah's and Derrick's conversation was very animated and such a glow on their faces. It reminded me of when Lucy and I were young. I looked at Lucy and she nodded; she was thinking the same thing. The lunch was excellent, and we talked a little about business. After dessert, Mr. Childs asked Sarah if she planned to go to college. When she said "Yes", Mr. Childs made a suggestion. Why didn't she attend the State college in their city. He had made a large contribution to the college to set up a course for design of houses and he could get her a scholarship. She could also work part time at the factory working with special customers on sales and design of kitchens. He even mentioned salary, which would be about three times what I had paid Sarah for working part time. He asked Sarah what she thought of this arrangement, and she said, "Fantastic!" He then went on to say that they owned a small apartment house near both the factory and the college. They just happened to have a small studio apartment that was empty and she could stay there. Mrs. Childs could check on her to make sure she was all right. Now it became obvious what the meeting was about.

Sarah would get a college education, a job for life and a proposal of marriage all in the same day. Mrs. Childs turned to me and Lucy and asked what we thought. I said I was overwhelmed, and all this was so sudden and Lucy agreed. Sarah was enthusiastic and could hardly wait to get started. We agreed that she could move and start on the job the first of the month after graduation. It would be hard with no children in the house and missing Sarah always laughing. But times do change, Sarah moved, and Lucy and I were enjoying our time together. The summer quickly passed, Emily graduated, got a job teaching second grade about thirty miles away. Dan was still in pre-med and Sarah was quickly settling into her new routine.

CHAPTER 3

THE HOLIDAYS

December comes and everyone will be home for Christmas. As usual Lucy is planning a big celebration and buying presents for everyone. On December 20th Lucy is still shopping for Christmas and on the way home, she was in a head on collision with a drunken driver. She is killed instantly. The drunken driver crossed over the center line on a curve and struck Lucy's car head on. He was also speeding and it was his third DWI arrest. I was devastated. I constantly thought how I would kill the SOB.

The funeral was a very trying affair. We had always planned on growing old together. The kids were able to cope better than I could. They had other parts to their lives, college, their studies, their friends and everything going on around them. But I had lost part of me. I would wake up in the middle of the night, in a cold sweat, and couldn't go back to sleep. I was a wreck and was getting worse. Finally I sought the help of a psychiatrist. I saw him three days a week for six months.

In the meantime, the drunk was convicted of Vehicular

Manslaughter and sentenced to three years in prison. I still planned to kill him when he was released.

After six months with the psychiatrist, he gave me his opinion. He could not help me. Sell my business and my house and go somewhere else and start a new life. I didn't like his assessment, but I was desperate. The transition took several months. I had always driven a pickup truck, so I was going to use the truck to travel in.

I said goodbye to the kids and decided I would go to Florida to visit my parents. After a few days, I decided to travel around Florida to look for a place to live. Nothing appealed to me and I went into Georgia, South Carolina, Mississippi, Alabama, Louisiana, Texas and was finally getting discouraged that I would ever find the right place. In December, three years after the accident I was in North Carolina. I stopped at a small motel on the shore of a lake. Tomorrow would be the anniversary of Lucy's death and I felt really terrible. I spent a very restless night, but woke up feeling calm and rested. I went next door to a little restaurant and had my usual breakfast. I walked outside to go to my truck and felt Lucy's spirit walking beside me. Lucy always had a large pocketbook and she would always place it on the seat between us. I could always feel it in my back when I drove. Today I could feel it more than I could remember. I felt so calm and peaceful with Lucy's spirit next to me, I decided I would drive slowly around the lake and enjoy the scenery. After about one hour, we came to a sign. It was so old you could not make out the name of the town. The only thing you could still read was population 9,400. I wanted to go look at the lake, but the town had been built away from the lake. We came to an old road that seemed to go toward the lake.

We passed a house that was very rundown, no paint, ready to fall down, when we came to a large sign. This old tobacco plantation "House and 30 acres for sale $10,000. See 1st national Bank." Talk about a wreck., windows broken, doors off the hinges, roof leaked, no electricity, no running water and a dump directly across the road. Of course, the 30 acres included the dump. I could see old tires, refrigerators, stoves, and even a couple of old davenports. It didn't smell bad, so I surmised no garbage. We looked at the back of the house and there was a huge outcropping of stone with a huge cave. The cave was large, probably 100 feet deep. The old driveway led down to the lake.

As we were walking down the driveway to the lake, Lucy turned to me and said, "Buy this place, you will be happy here." Lucy had never been wrong on major decisions. We walked on down to the lake and there were the remains of an old dock. Lucy walked out onto the dock and disappeared. I walked back to the truck, feeling calmer than I had felt in years. It didn't take long to find the bank, locate the president and sit down to make the deal. I told him I didn't want the portion with the dump, so we added a paragraph to the sale contract to that effect. He told me that all the papers were in order and we could close in three days. I called my bank and told them to transfer $50,000 to my account in this bank.

I asked about a trailer dealer nearby and he said, "Yes". He was his friend, so he called him and said I would be over to see him. He happened to have a used 20 foot travel trailer on the lot, and he could deliver it that afternoon and set it up. I then contacted the power company. They first told me they would have to get permission of the people who owned the right away to set the poles. I told them I owned the right away, so that problem was solved. I would have to pay for the poles and the boxes. Installation could be done in a week or so. Next came the water. I went to the town hall and they really didn't care whether I had water or not. The superintendent finally told me if I put in the line, they would hook it up for me. There was a yearly charge, so no meter was involved.

The next stop was the Home depot. This was not a large store and their stock was limited. I asked about 2" plastic pipe and they had that. I then asked about a backhoe to dig the trench, and they had a small one that would work. They also had the fittings I would need. I then asked about cedar shakes. "We have two bundles in stock; how many do you need?" "Probably 20 or 25 bundles." "We can get any amount in two days." I opened an account and bought a small generator and a couple of gas cans. I stopped at the grocery store and bought some cereal, bread, peanut butter and jelly and some milk. I then stopped at the filling station and got gas for the generator. And then back to the site to show the dealer where to put the trailer.

It has been a busy day, I spent time with Lucy, and got started on my new life. I hadn't felt so calm and peaceful for years. For the next three days I was very busy taking care of the odds and ends, ordering a telephone and getting to know the town. I also planned how I would start the remodeling project, the tools and material that I would need. I couldn't order anything until the closing. I did start one project, I remembered, when I had done a job replacing a shake roof, years ago. There were wasp nests and hornets in the attic. So I bought six cans of wasp bombs and set them off in the attic, hoping to kill any wasps or hornets.

I also examined the property more closely. The cave intrigued me. It showed signs that people had been there. Most of the land was across the road that went to the lake and was taken up by the dump and a swale that was part of the lake. Originally the slave quarters were in an area close to the house and this was still a colored area. The houses were very run down, no running water, no sewers, no paint, out houses and junk everywhere. I wondered why people would live in houses this bad.

After checking my house, I wondered why I would remodel the

house, instead of building a new one. One fact remained, if I remodeled the old house, I would have a project that would take three or four years. That might be therapy for my mind. The next three days passed quickly, and the day to close had arrived.

I was at the bank when it opened, and was waiting for the president of the bank. The president was a very likable fellow about 5'10", weight about 175 lbs. with slightly graying hair, well dressed and spoke very slowly. I liked him at once and thought we should be friends. We quickly signed all the papers and I made out the check. I had a whole list of questions, who owned the property? How long had it been empty? What was the cave used for? It had been empty for over thirty years. The owner was Miz Rose Mayers, who was a direct descendant of the original owners and was the matriarch of the town. She knew everything that was going on and help make all the major decisions in the town. The cave was where the slaves used to meet and stay during bad storms and hurricanes. The president also told me that everyone knew Miz Rose and everyone called her that. If I wanted any other information, just ask.

I left the bank and headed for Home depot. I had a list of tools needed, lumber to build the scaffold and cedar shakes for the roof , and a tarp to cover the roof when I removed the old shingles. They had already ordered enough shakes to do ten squares, so I ordered 15 squares more. They would deliver the whole order right after lunch. I also ordered a picnic table and benches. I then went home to wait for the delivery. I had lunch and got out the generator for power. The electricity was not in yet, so I needed the generator to run the saw. About 1:00 pm the truck arrived and was quickly unloaded. Everything was placed in the house.

CHAPTER 4

THE BEGINNING OF REMODELING

Since the house was only one story, the scaffold was not very high. I decided the height was about knee high to the eaves. I put up the scaffold and then put on the tarp to cover the hole when I took off the shingles. I tacked on a few lath to hold the tarp on in case the wind came up. I knew the easiest way to remove the old shakes was with a garden spade, so I removed the bottom three courses to start. There are always nails that don't come out with the shingles. I pulled the nails and dropped them in a pail.

I hadn't gone very far until I saw a small package wrapped in oil cloth and tied with a string. I couldn't wait to open this package. I cut the string, unwrapped the oil cloth and found a small wooden box. Curiosity sure set in now and I opened the box. Inside were five letters, addressed to a Miss. The names were faded but were still legible, so I put them in the box, wrapped them in the oil cloth and retied the string. I took them down to the trailer for safe keeping.

I then started installing the new shakes. The first course is doubled making sure the top layer covered the cracks in the first layer. The second and each succeeding course is 5" higher. To maintain this, a line is stretched from end to end, so the 5" distance is maintained. Since the new shakes may be slippery, cleats are installed about every four feet. These are usually 2 x 4's and shingles are nailed to the 2 x 4's, a minimum amount of overlap, about one inch, and then in place. These are left on until the roof is completed, then the shingles are sawed off even with the rest of the shingles in the row.

At the end of the day I had completed the first two courses and had removed the next five courses and pulled the nails. I brought the tarp down to cover the open area, tacked it down and quit for the day. It was time for a handyman dinner and bed. Tomorrow is another day.

CHAPTER 5

MEETING THE PEOPLE

The next morning I got started early. I felt very calm and looking forward to the job. I carried several bundles of shakes up to the scaffold and I was ready to start. Progress was very good until noon, so I decided to stop for lunch. I planned to cut the lunch short so I was having peanut butter and jelly sandwiches and milk to drink, and then it happened.

My first visitor was like an apparition. He was a young colored kid about nine years old, filthy dirty, long hair, ragged clothes. I thought to myself, "This kid has no parents. No parent would let their kid get in this condition." I asked if he had lunch and he said, "No", so I made him a peanut butter and jelly sandwich. Evidently he hadn't eaten for days; he jammed the whole sandwich in his mouth without chewing it. I asked if he would like another sandwich and he said "Yes". I made him another and told him he had to eat this one slowly and take time to chew it. I got him a paper cup and poured him a cup of milk. I asked him his name and he told me "Bay Lee". And then he asked if he could have a sandwich for his brother and sister. I suggested he go get his brother and sister; they might like two sandwiches. He quickly went to the old ramshackle house just up the road and brought back his brother and sister. They looked every bit decrepit as Bay and just as hungry. The boy was called Benny and was seven; the girl was Jada and was six. I made them each a sandwich and poured them a glass of milk. I told them they should eat slowly. I also made Bay another sandwich. Since I was running out of bread, I could only give Benny and Jada another half sandwich.

I was thinking to myself that tomorrow is Christmas, and the kids are hungry. This is the first time in three years that I thought about anyone except myself. I asked the kids if they would like to join me tomorrow for lunch. I poured the rest of the milk in their cups and they finished that and left for home.

I quickly jumped in the truck and went to the grocery store. I didn't want to run out again, so I bought four Handyman turkey dinners, two gallons of milk, two loaves of bread and a large jar of peanut butter and one of jelly. Cookies for dessert. I had cereal in case they should come for breakfast. I didn't feel like working this afternoon, so just covered the job with the tarp.

Since I didn't have a phone yet, I found a pay phone and called each of the kids and told them what was happening and my address. And I wished them all "Merry Christmas". They were all surprised at this since I hadn't bothered with Christmas for the past three years. My parents were called and wished the same. Christmas was going to be like Christmas this year. I awoke Christmas morning, got dressed and decided I would have breakfast out at the picnic table. The kids were all sitting on their front porch, I guess waiting for me. I motioned for them to come on over. I got out the paper cups and bowls, the cereal and milk and brought them out to the picnic table. The kids didn't seem to be so ravenous this morning, but we each had two bowls of cereal. They told me their mother's welfare check hadn't come yet.

They talked more today, but I still didn't get much information. I told them I would have lunch ready at 1:00 pm. They said they would be here.

About 12:30 I started cooking the Hungryman dinners and while they were cooking, I set out a pan of warm water, soap and towels. This would probably be a first in their young lives. When they came over at 1:00, I told them before we could eat they had to wash their hands and face. This didn't take long, and it wasn't very complete, but it was a start.

The kids had trouble with the sliced turkey, so I cut it up for them. Boy, did they go to town on those meals. While they were eating, I knew I had to figure out how to get them to bathe. I didn't have running water yet and electricity or gas to heat it with. I had been advised when I went to the town hall that the inspector checked both the plumbing and the electricity. If I wanted the jobs to pass, I had better have his brother do the work. I knew this arrangement would cost at least 100% more, so I decided to find an alternative. Tomorrow would be Sunday and I had no place to get information.

On Sunday we had peanut butter and jelly sandwiches and milk to drink. Washing their hands and faces were now a must, but I noticed most of the dirt went on the towels, so I had to have a washer and dryer hookup.

Monday morning arrived and at 9:00 am I was at the bank. The president of the bank already knew I had the Lee kids for Christmas dinner. After the pleasantries, we got down to business about an inspector for plumbing and electricity. He knew the instructor for the BOCES program that also had a plumbing company and installed electrical and septic systems. He recommended him highly and said he knew he would be reasonable. He offered to call him, which he did and introduced me. He already knew I had bought the place, and was very familiar with it. I asked him how soon he could do the work. I would like it right away. "Would you like it done over the Christmas vacation?" "Wonderful!" "I'll get together a crew and be there tomorrow morning."

I then phoned the power company to see when they planned to start. The supervisor of installation informed me that the crew would be there today and complete the job over the Christmas holidays. I then went to Home Depot to see if they could build me a small outbuilding to house a shower, hot water heater, toilet, washer and dryer. They already had plans for a 12'x 15' building containing all these features with a concrete floor with all the plumbing and electrical details.

I was amazed at the progress I had made and it wasn't even lunch time yet. I took the plans with me and headed for home. When I arrived, I found two young colored men waiting for me. They were both quite husky, about five feet eight or nine, and about 165 pounds. They looked like they would be good workers. They were both about thirty and looking for a job. I asked if they were roofers and they said "No", but they could do it if I showed them how. So then I asked them how much pay they expected. They replied, "Would $10 a day be all right?" I had always paid my employees $15 to $18 an hour to start, so I was surprised at this. I told them I would start them at $8 an hour. If they weren't good workers, I would fire them; if they were good workers, I would pay them more. When did they want to start? They said "right away".

Since I didn't have any paperwork to fill out, I asked their names. Nate and John were cousins and turned out to be excellent workers. We went up on the scaffold and I showed them how to remove the old shingles, how to stretch the line and to install the new ones. They were told to be sure each shake had a nail on each side and none in the middle. Be sure to cover the cracks in the former layer and be sure the nails would be covered by the next course. It was clear that their lack of experience would be no handicap. Within a few minutes they were doing fine, so I decided to go to the village hall to get the necessary paperwork. When I got back, they had made good progress and I decided to wait for quitting time to fill out the papers. Just before 5:00 pm I told them to cover the hole with the tarp and come down to fill out the paperwork.

Much to my surprise, neither of them could read, so I asked the questions and filled out the paperwork for them. They could both sign their name, but had never attended school. I asked them why and they told me that the people in the area didn't allow blacks to go to school. I now could understand the appearance of Bay, when I first met him and the condition of his brother and sister. I sent Nate and John home and told them to be here at 7:30 in the morning.

This was going to be a busy day. I was up at 6:00 am. At about 7:00 the septic tank contractor arrived with his crew and we discussed the lines to the septic tank and the addition of the new building. First, the hole for the septic tank, as it would be arriving about 10:00. Since the soil was sandy, it did not take long to dig the hole, and the man on the backhoe was an expert. Nate and John arrived and I turned them over to the contractor. About this time, the power company arrived with all their trucks and poles. They started their job. Then the crew from Home Depot arrived to put in the concrete pad for their building. Confusion was everywhere. The truck with the gravel for the leach field arrived, then the 1,000 gallon septic tank.

The contractor was right on the ball and kept everything in order. He laid out the drain lines from the trailer, the house and for the new building. Then he asked me about the water lines. Since this wasn't in yet, I used his expertise and I contracted with him to put in the new water line. The Home Depot crew had brought the copper pipe for the water line and the plastic pipe for the drains. This was roughed in before the concrete was poured. The forms were built, the concrete poured and worked smooth. They were all through by 4:00 pm. The concrete would have to set for 48 hours before they could start on the building.

The power company had the poles all set and they gave me the specs for the temporary box. They will return tomorrow to put up the transformer and the lines and hook up the temporary box. I will have to go to Home Depot to pick it up. I will also pick up the two inch plastic pipe for the water line and all the connections. I will also put in the connections at Bay's house, in case they ever decide to put in water. This has been a very busy day.

When the kids came over for dinner, we had to settle for sandwiches and milk. Luckily, I have some bologna to make sandwiches. Not much but better than nothing. After eating, I went to Home Depot to pick up my supplies. Tomorrow will be another busy day.

Next morning, up at 6:00 am, by 7:30 the contractor and his crew have arrived and we are ready to start. The septic tank was set yesterday, so today is the distribution box and the leach field. The most time consuming part was putting the gravel in the leach field. We had plenty of help, so this didn't take long. We put the felt paper to cover the pipes and then the dirt on top. By the end of the day, everything is covered up and ready to use. The power company has strung the wires, put up the transformer and hooked up the temporary box. I will be able to plug in my extension cord and have electricity in the trailer. Tomorrow we will put in the water line. The line only has to be 18 inches deep so the trench doesn't take long to dig. It is about 350 feet to the main connection, so we start there. We leave extra plastic pipe for the connection at the end.

When we get to Bay's house, we put in the connections and a valve so the hookup would be easy. Then we put this in a box to keep the valve and connections clean and free of dirt. On to my section and we make the connections to the trailer and leave the trench open to the house and the new building. I turn off all the valves and go down to the town hall to get the water hooked up. I had bought all the fittings needed to hook it up. The man came with me to the hook up spot, and then told me he would have to go get the material to make the hookup and he would be back in the morning. I told him I already had the parts, and he said he could not use them as they might be inferior quality.

The next day he showed up with the same parts purchased at Home Depot. Finally we were hooked up and I had water to the trailer and was hooked up to the septic tank. The connections were made to the new building and were ready to be turned on.

Tomorrow is New Year's. I had really made progress in ten days and was feeling wonderful. Before we finished, the contractor called me aside and told me he would like to hire Nate and John and teach them to be electricians and plumbers. He didn't have any men who were as good workers as they were. I told him they could not read and he said that would not matter. He would like them by April 1, as that was the beginning of his busy season. I told him I would talk it over with them and recommend they work for him. We all took New Year's day off, so I got Handyman dinners for the kids and myself. We had the usual cereal for breakfast and I told the kids to come over about 1:00 for lunch. I felt that I had really made progress, not only on the property, but also the way I felt about myself.

When the kids arrived, I had the Handyman dinners ready and we ate. While we were eating, I asked Bay "Can you read?" and he said, "No, hain't never bin to school." This would be a good time to discuss my future plans. I told them about the new building and we would have hot water and a shower. They had to take a shower every day. I would take them to the thrift store and buy them all decent clothes. We would have a washer and dryer, so they could have clean clothes every day. We would get their hair cut. I would also get some books and get Bay started, so he could read. I would teach Bay and he could teach Ben and Jada. They were very anxious about the new clothes, but fearful about the showers. We would start this as soon as the new building was completed and everything installed. I realized how much extra work I was planning and decided I needed some help. But who? First things first. I would go see Nate and John and discuss the contractor's offer. Nate and John lived next door to each other and John's wife always brought them lunch. So to John's house I went.

Both Nate and John were sitting on the front porch of this ramshackle house, and John's older brother, Sam was there showing his gold front tooth. Sam is bigger than Nate or John. Sam is a couple of inches taller and probably weighs about two hundred and twenty pounds. But his smile is a yard wide and always shows his gold tooth. . They welcomed me and then I told them about the contractor and his offer. After they had learned the trades, they could get a license and go into business for themselves. John said, "But what about your work?"

I replied, "Oh, I will find somebody else."

"What about Sam?"

I turned to Sam and said, "Are you as good a worker as John?"

"Much better", said Sam as he smiled a smile a yard wide, showing his gold front tooth. It turns out Sam has an old dump truck and he makes a few dollars occasionally hauling stuff.

About this time John's wife, Ida, brought out some tea. Not hot, not cold, but wet! She is smart, about five feet five inches, weight about 125 pounds and very trim looking. I trusted her completely I asked her if she would like to work a few hours every day helping with the kids doing their washing, fixing their lunch and making sure they took a shower. She was overjoyed and didn't even ask the pay. I told her she could start when the new building was completed and we had everything installed. I am always amazed by how easily the problems are solved, as though someone was helping.

Tomorrow will be another busy day. Up at 6 am and we have our cereal. About 7:30 Nate, John and Sam arrive. They put the shakes on the scaffold to get started. Shortly after 8:00 the Home Depot crew arrived and started putting up the building. The concrete is hard, but has not cured enough to put down tile, so I have them put down a sub floor. Tomorrow will be the tile, the next day start installing the toilet, shower, sink, hot water tank and washer and dryer. Everything is roughed in, the drains, water and electricity, so installation should go smoothly.

At lunch time, the kids and I are having our sandwiches when an old pickup truck drove up and two young men about 25 years old, got out, strode up to the picnic table, as though they owned the place, and wanted to see the owner. I told them I was the owner. They immediately became very belligerent and informed me that whenever anybody hired a n----- in this town they hired a white man to supervise the n-----, and they were here to get the job. I told them I had no openings and my men did not need a supervisor. They then informed me that anybody who didn't play by their rules could expect a fire in their building. I steamed at their attitude in the beginning and now I had really had it.

"If I ever have a fire around here, I will hunt you down and break every damn bone in your body." By now I was shouting. "Do you understand?"

He barely answered "Yes".

"The answer is 'Yes Sir', unless you want me to start right now."

Loud and clear, "Yes Sir."

And I turned to the other man and said, "Do you understand?"

"*Yes Sir* ", loud and clear.

The two got up, walked to the truck and drove away. After they had gone, Bay turned to me and said, "I don't think you liked those fellows very well!" I replied, "Sometimes you have to tell a person who is the boss!" Bay learned his first big lesson today.

When Ida brought the men's lunch, I asked her if she would take the kids down to the thrift store and buy them each three outfits and if she had enough money left, to go to the shoe store and buy them shoes and socks. She said she would, so after lunch they started out. I gave Ida a fifty dollar bill to pay for the stuff. About two hours later a deputy sheriff drove up to see me. They had arrested Ida, because they thought she had stolen the fifty dollars. The manager of the thrift store had called them and reported the fifty dollar bill. I had never met the sheriff or any of his deputies, but that was about to change. I got in the truck to go see the sheriff and the farther I drove, the madder I got. By the time I arrived, I was really steaming. When I walked into the office, Ida and the kids were sitting on chairs in the waiting room. I asked Ida what had happened. She said that when she went to pay for the clothes with the fifty dollar bill, the manager had called the sheriff. I then demanded to see the sheriff.

The sheriff was huge, at least six feet and probably about two hundred and fifty pounds and exuded authority. He had a pleasant personality and seemed to fill the shoes of the sheriff to perfection.

We sat down in his office and I told him I expected him to fire the deputy, that when I sent an employee to do a job for me, I expected them to be treated with respect. The sheriff was very cordial, didn't get excited, and gave me a very detailed explanation.

First, it wasn't the deputy's fault, <u>he </u>had taken the call and sent the deputy on the call.

"The deputy was one of his best deputies and was only following orders.

Next, black people never have a fifty dollar bill in this town and when this happened, it was very suspicious." He then apologized. Then asked, "What can I do to resolve the matter?"

I told him, "I think the deputy should apologize to Ida, take her back to the thrift store, tell the manager, it was OK. And also tell the manager to give Ida a damn good price on the clothes. Then he should drive Ida and the kids back to my place."

The sheriff then said, "Man, you sure drive a hard bargain!"

So I said, "Maybe you should let me tell him!"

The sheriff agreed, so he asked the deputy to come in. When the deputy came in and was seated, I explained to him.

"I come from up north and we treated blacks as people. He had a choice; he could apologize to Ida, take her back to the thrift store, talk to the manager and make sure she got a good price or I would do my best to get him fired."

"Man, you sure don't leave me much choice. I have a family to support and this is the only job I ever had, so I will do it."

I think both the sheriff and the deputy gained a new viewpoint today.

The deputy must have done a good job on the manager, because Ida came home with twice the amount of clothes she was supposed to buy and she was charged only five dollars. When Ida came back, she told me that both the sheriff and the deputy had apologized to her and that she had never been treated by a white person as they treated her. I asked her to take the kids tomorrow to buy shoes and socks. Then the next day she could start her regular job.

That afternoon I went downtown and bought a dozen towels and wash cloths, shampoo, bath soap and powder. Tomorrow we start the transformation!

CHAPTER 6

NEW BEGINNING

The morning started early. Nate, John and Sam had finished the side of the roof they were working on, so we had to move the scaffold to the other side, which had the chimney and a valley. I had to explain how to put the metal in the valley and how to install the flashing around the chimney. I also found out they were not using rules to measure. Since they couldn't read, they didn't trust them. I told them it was absolutely necessary to learn how to use them. I asked if they could count; that was no problem. I then showed them 1 and 2 and through 12, and then the one foot mark, then 2 and 3. They asked what the small marks were. I asked them how many quarters in a one. And how many quarters in a dollar? They all knew it was four. And then I said, "If there are four quarters in one dollar, how many quarters in a one?" They all realized it was four, so I showed them the quarter inch lines and said we would have another lesson tomorrow.

Ida came about 10:00 to take the kids to buy shoes. She had to call them over as they had gone home after breakfast. I told Ida the kids couldn't wear the shoes until after their shower. Since they had new clothes and new shoes, they could hardly wait. We had a quick lunch and then off to the new building. First I had to show them how everything worked. The first item was the toilet, how it worked and how to flush it; and then the shower, how it worked and how to adjust the hot and cold. Ida was told that she was in charge of the building and she could schedule everything as she pleased. If she had any dirty clothes, she should bring them tomorrow and I would show her how the washer and dryer worked. She needed to know how much shampoo to use and I then instructed her that I wanted the kids clean. All the old dirt had to be removed from the top of their heads to the bottom of their feet. About two hours later, Ida brought the kids out, clean with new clothes, shoes and socks. What a difference!!

Since I needed a haircut, I decided to take them to the barber. The barber didn't recognize the Lee kids and asked who they were. I told him that these were the Lee kids and introduced him to each one. I was first with the haircut and then Bay. My haircut was no problem, but when we got to Bay, we had to decide what and how much. We finally decided on a short brush cut. No combing and easy to keep clean. Ben came next, the same thing, but when we got to Jada, I had to take the barber's advice and give her the current style. After he had finished, I asked, "How much?" He said, "Four dollars; I am charging you for the haircut. If you can do this much for the Lee kids, I can certainly cut their hair for free." I thanked him and told him I certainly appreciated it. They now looked like normal everyday kids. I dropped them off at their house and drove on home.

Within a few minutes Bay and Jada came running over to the trailer. Bay told me his mother's boyfriend tried to do Jada. They had received the welfare check and he was half drunk. Within a couple of minutes he was at the door. He banged on the door and when I opened it, he demanded that Jada come home. I just stepped out the door and told him in no uncertain terms, "You drunken SOB, if you ever touch that little girl, I will personally castrate you." With that he turned and walked back to Bay's house. I didn't trust him, so I had Ida take Jada home with her to stay the night.

The next morning when the boys came for breakfast, Bay told me that the boyfriend had beaten up his mother. I decided right away to go talk to the sheriff. On the way to the sheriff's office, I stopped at the drug supply store and asked if they had a knife used for castration. Of course, they had several styles, one even had a holster, so I chose that one and immediately put in on my belt. Then I went on to the sheriff's office. The sheriff was in and invited me into his office. I told him the problem and he said this was not the first time, but Bay's mother would never prefer charges, so he was powerless to do anything. He then noticed the holster and asked what it was for. I told him that was a castration knife. I had told the drunken SOB that if he touched Jada, I would castrate him. He suddenly started cleaning the wax out of his ears with his little finger and told me he couldn't hear a darn word I was saying!

After awhile he agreed to go to Bay's house and talk with Bay's mother. As before, she wouldn't prefer charges, so I asked the sheriff if I could prefer the charges. He said I could, but he didn't know how the judge would view it. So the sheriff arrested the boyfriend and put him in jail. He asked me to appear before the judge tomorrow morning.

When the judge was in his robe, he was all business. He was very stern and knowledgeable about the whole case. He was also familiar with my association with the kids and their progress. He knew the defendant never worked and lived off the welfare checks and spent most of it on booze. The judge didn't waste any time sentencing the defendant to six months in jail. I asked if I could make a suggestion. The judge agreed.

"I suggest that the defendant mow the weeds and brush along the road instead of just sitting in jail waiting for his next meal."

The defendant immediately jumped to his feet and shouted, "I won't do it; I won't work."

The judge looked to me for an answer, so I suggested, "No work, no eat and if he starves to death, we will take him to the cemetery and bury him." That was exactly what the sentence was, although the judge left off the part about the cemetery.

The sheriff then took the defendant back to the jail..

When the judge took off his robe, he thanked me for my suggestion and said I was a big help in the case.

Then with a smile on his face and a twinkle in his eye, he asked how the kids were doing. He had already heard about the kids showering, their haircuts and about Ida being arrested and how that was handled. He knew everything that was going on as well as I did. From the moment he took off his robe, his personality changed completely. He was friendly and smiling, and you didn't really notice he was only about five feet four inches tall and a little pudgy, not much, but a little. Hair was beginning to gray and a little thin at the temples. But his personality made up for all that. I knew we would be friends.

The next day the defendant was escorted by a deputy to the roadside to begin his sentence. He was furnished a scythe, an axe and a gallon jug of water. He sat all day the first day, even when the deputy was eating his lunch, and made no effort to work. The next day, after the deputy finished his lunch, the defendant picked up the scythe and started cutting weeds. But his life of leisure and drinking left him in poor physical condition and little strength. So the first couple of days he didn't accomplish much. By the end of the first month, eating three meals a day, he had regained enough strength to work all day.

With the boyfriend out of the way, Jada returned home, and I did away with the castration knife. Ida was doing real well with the new building, making sure the kids got a daily bath and had clean clothes every day. She had also joined the shower every day group. Nate, John and Sam asked if they could shower and I told them to ask Ida. She was in charge. I had wondered about the kids' teeth, so I made an appointment for all of us. I was surprised the kids' teeth were in pretty good condition, only a couple of minor cavities for each one. I had the dentist explain how to brush their teeth and stopped on the way home to buy toothpaste and a dozen tooth brushes. I knew that Ida, Nate, John and Sam would join the group brushing their teeth.

On Saturday afternoon after Nate, John and Sam had stopped working, I asked John if he knew Mrs. Mayers, and he said, "Oh, you mean Miz Rose, everybody knows Miz Rose." I asked if he would go see her for me and tell her I would like to see her at my place. He said, "Sure" and off he went. In a few minutes he was back and said she would be here the next day at 1:00.

Before she arrived, I made a large pitcher of iced tea and got out some lemon and sugar. At one minute before one o'clock Mrs. Mayers arrived in her Lincoln Town car. It was several years old, but it looked like it left the showroom yesterday. I met her at her car and said, "Welcome, Mrs. Mayers."

She looked at me and said, "Everyone calls me Miz Rose."

So I replied, "But I don't know you that well, Mrs. Mayers." So we went over to the picnic table and sat down, as I poured the tea and asked "sugar or lemon?"

"Lemon, please." And then I told her, "I have something to show you."

I showed her the box wrapped in oil cloth that I had found in the attic. She untied the string and took off the oil cloth to open the box.

When she saw the letters and to whom they were addressed, a look of amazement came over her face.

She asked, "Where did you find them?"

I told her, "In the attic. If I hadn't replaced the roof, I would never have found them."

She asked "Did you read them?"

"No, there might be something personal in them."

She then told me "They were addressed to my great grandmother before she was married." She then asked, "Would you accept five hundred dollars for the letters?"

"No, Mrs. Mayers, I didn't ask you over here to sell you something. I don't need your money, but I thought they might have some historical significance for your family. They never belonged to me; they are yours." I then changed the subject and asked her, "Do you know the Lee kids?"

"Of course, many people have tried to help the kids, but no one had figured how to help, until you came along.

Their father was a wonderful man, but he was killed in an accident about three years ago. All the colored people in this area are descendants of the slaves for the plantation. Many have never moved away. I suspect some of them might be my relatives, but I don't know which ones. The town is built on the fields where they used to plant tobacco. The cave in the big rock was where they used to go when they had a hurricane. The town has never accepted them, even though they were here before the town. No one has ever been interested in the place, and I wondered many times what brought you here."

"That is a long story."

"I would be interested, if you would like to tell me."

"OK! I will make it short as I can."

I then proceeded to tell her of my life with Lucy, the three children and what they were doing. Then about Lucy being killed by a drunk driver and its effect on me. About my seeing a psychiatrist and his diagnosis and wandering over the south for over two years.

"Then on December 20 I was on the other side of the lake and when I went to my car, I was met by Lucy's spirit and she suggested we drive around the lake. We turned off the main road and wanted to drive down to the lake. Then we came to the sign that said the old plantation was for sale.

Lucy's spirit said to me, "Buy this place, you will be happy here."

We then walked down to the lake, Lucy walked out on the dock and disappeared. So I went back to the bank and made arrangements to buy the place.

We had talked for over three hours and the iced tea was long gone. She turned to me and said, "I think we know each other well enough so you can call me Miz Rose. I will join you every year on December 20th at one o'clock, so we can have tea together."

"Only if you call me Gee, and I hope we get together before then." "Why don't you come to my place on Thursday night about 7:00? Fred, the bank president will be there and the judge. You have met both and we will play a little gin." And so started the gin games that lasted for many years.

After Miz Rose left, I went into the trailer to answer the phone. It was Emily and she had good news. She wanted to get married and asked if I would come home to be part of the wedding. I told her I wouldn't miss it for the world. She only wanted a small wedding; they hadn't set a firm date, but were thinking early June. Dan and Sarah would be out of school. I told her to let me know the date and I would be there. Then I asked her if they had a house. She told me they had already bought one. I was certainly happy that Emily was getting married and I would be able to see all the kids again.

I was so excited that I had trouble sleeping, but Monday morning arrived. The roof was almost finished and we could start on the inside. Many of the rooms were quite small, so I had planned to move some walls. I planned on doing this first, before doing windows and doors, so I would know they were in the right place.

Ida came early this morning and wanted to know if Bay's mother could take a shower. I told her she was in charge of that building and she could make the decision, but I would be very happy to see Bay's mother take an interest in her looks. I then gave Ida $40 and told her to go down to the thrift store and buy her some clothes. She said she would do that today.

About 11 am the mailman drove up. Usually all I got were bills and junk mail, but today he had a registered letter. It was from the State and instructed me to clean up the old dump. They would allow me a year to do it. I wasn't too disturbed because in the sales contract I had specified that I did not want the dump. I decided I would mention it to the judge on Thursday night.

On Tuesday afternoon Bay's mother took her shower and put on clean clothes. What a difference! She looked human again. When the roof was finished, all the old shingles were lying on the ground, so I had Sam bring his truck to haul the debris to the dump. I called and found out that he would need a permit to dump the debris. I gave Sam the money to pay for the permit. The dump was about twenty miles away and was the county landfill. This was where all the garbage and debris was supposed to be disposed of. It took Sam most of the day to make the trip and I was surprised he completed the trip at all, due to the age of the old truck.

I had drawn up a plan showing the finished layout of the rooms. The kitchen and the pantry were okay and the living room was in the right place, but the windows had to be moved. The bedrooms were all small and there was no place for the two bathrooms that I planned to install, so we had to move some walls. Some of the floor boards had rotted out due to leaks in the roof and I managed to buy some from a used lumber dealer. Naturally where the floor boards were rotted, the sills below were also rotted, so we had to replace them. While the floor was removed, we brought in the drain lines and water lines for the kitchen and bathrooms. Since all this work was new to Nate, John and Sam, progress was slow. Fortunately the house had been raised about three feet off the ground, so we didn't have termite damage. We quit early Thursday, so I could get ready to go to Miz Rose's.

I arrived at 7 pm and Fred and the judge were already there. They were having hot tea and cookies. Their first question, "How are you doing?" I explained about the order from the State to clean up the dump, but I was not worried because I had said in the sales contract that I did not want the dump. I looked at the judge for his opinion and he told me, "Yes, you could probably win a decision, but it would cost you at least ten times as much to win as it would cost to clean it up. I would say, clean it up."

Miz Rose then asked how the Lee kids were doing. "Fine" "They are eating three meals a day, they take a shower every day, they have had a haircut, been to the dentist and brush their teeth every day, but I can't figure how to get them an education. Oh, by the way, Bay's mother is also showering every day and has clean clothes." "Oh, we knew that", Miz Rose says. So then we started playing gin. I lost three dollars and twenty cents the first night, but enjoyed the first night of relaxation I had known for years.

The next day I had a sign made and put up at the dump that said, "No dumping allowed". I called the power company to put up two poles at the dump with a floodlight on each pole, but not to hook up any power to the lights. They were instructed to leave a loose wire hanging from the light. I called Fred at the bank to see who installed and maintained their cameras. I then called the man to see if he could install what I wanted. Could he install two cameras on telephone poles that would be battery operated, have a motion switch that would turn on with any motion in the vicinity and work with super sensitive film that would work in the dark? No problem so far; could he also leave a wire dangling from the camera to make people think it had to be hooked to electricity? "No problem, but when did I want it installed?" I told him I would call as soon as the poles were set. The power company had told me they would set the poles as soon as a crew was available, probably within the next two weeks.

When we started moving walls, I realized that we should also install the electrical lines, so I called my friend at BOCES, who had put in the septic system, to come over and put in the entrance line and switch box. He worked with Nate and John and explained the whole procedure to them. He was also looking for the day they would start working for him. He asked if Nate and John could attend the current BOCES course on electrical installation. He would pay the BOCES fee. Nate and John agreed, so he filled out the papers on the spot and took them with him.

That evening I called Sarah to see how she was doing and gave her the dimensions of the kitchen and pantry, the two bathrooms and the location of the water lines and drain lines. I also wanted her to arrange shipment of the cupboards, sinks and toilets. She asked when I would be ready and I said maybe in about three weeks. She said she would call back in two weeks to see how I was progressing. She also said she was looking forward to Emily's wedding and would see me there. This was Sarah's last year in college and she was to graduate in June. I kept wondering what her plans were, but was reluctant to ask.

Thursday rolled around almost before I realized, and I was on the way to Miz Rose's house for cards. Every day I checked the dump to see if anybody was dumping new stuff, absolutely nothing. When I arrived at Miz Rose's house, they were having hot tea and key lime pie. I had had key lime pie before, but this was the best by far. Miz Rose had made two pies and there was half a pie left that she set aside for me to take home. Before we started playing cards, Miz Rose mentioned the kids' education. She had found a solution. She had located a retired teacher, who needed a little extra income and would tutor the kids for six days a week for forty dollars a week. It was evident that the three of them had discussed this before, because each pledged ten dollars a week and naturally I pledged the other ten dollars. Miz Rose said Mrs. Sims knew the kids and wanted to help. I was to drive the kids to her house every day and they were to start the following Monday. I was so elated over this good news that I couldn't concentrate on the cards. Before the night was over, I had lost seven dollars and forty cents. I don't think I had a gin all night, but I did have half a delicious key lime pie to take home.

The next morning when the kids came for breakfast, I told them the good news. I knew Bay wanted to learn, so I impressed him that he had to be the smartest and help Ben and Jada. I told him I wanted him to be the smartest boy in town, and he promised me he would.

When Ida arrived, I told her the kids were going to be tutored. She was very happy and would change her working hours. Anytime I couldn't drive the kids, she would do it.

Moving the walls was really a messy job. We had to tear off the old lathe and plaster to get to the studs. To make it easier, Sam parked his truck next to the porch and as we tore down the lathe and plaster, we dumped it into the truck. We finished tearing down the plaster by mid-afternoon. When some of Sam's neighbors heard that Sam had a permit for the dump, they asked him if the next time he went to the dump, would he take some items for them. Since he didn't have a load, Sam spent the rest of the afternoon collecting the rest of his load. He would go to the dump the first thing in the morning. In the meantime Nate, John and I moved the walls. Instead of lathe and plaster, we put up sheetrock on the new walls. There were many holes in the old plaster, so we mixed up the plaster to patch these holes. Patching the holes takes several days, as the first coat is thick and has to dry two or three days. Then the next coat takes at least a day to dry before the finish coat is put on. We spent over a week changing the walls and patching the plaster.

This week at Miz Rose's was uneventful, no great changes, nothing new. We had egg salad sandwiches and hot tea, and I lost only 80 cents.

Nate and John are getting good practical information at BOCES, so I let them do the basic stuff on the electrical wiring. The plaster patching is going well and should be dry enough for the finish coat. Yesterday I talked to Mrs. Sims, who is tutoring the kids, to see how they were doing. She said she was surprised at their progress. The kids were very eager to learn and especially Bay, who is very quick to learn.

The power company put up the two poles today and the foreman came over to talk to me. "Are you sure you don't want the lights hooked up?" "Positive", I told him, but I didn't give him the reason. I called the camera man and told him that the poles were in and he could install the cameras.

Sarah called tonight and wanted to know when I would be ready for the cupboards. I told her by the end of next week I would be ready. She said she would ship the stuff out right away., I went to Miz Rose's Thursday night as usual and thought I had a lot of good news to report, but found out they knew more than I did. They must have had daily briefings on the kids' progress. They also asked about Sam hauling stuff to the dump and thought maybe he should buy a newer truck and plan to make a couple of trips to the dump every week. I will talk it over with Sam. There were donuts and hot tea tonight and I even won $1.10. I had the feeling tonight that I had three partners helping me.

The camera man put up the cameras today and as I had requested, left some loose wire hanging from the cameras. I talked to Sam about a different truck and he said he would have to buy a newer truck, if he found one he could afford. He thought he could find enough junk to make two trips to the dump every week. I watched my dump every day to see if any new material ended up there. So far nothing.

It was Thursday night again and cards at Miz Rose's. They asked what Sam had said about a different truck and I told them that Sam was willing if he found one that he could afford. They then told me that the county was having an auction and was selling five trucks which they thought would be sold cheap. They even gave me a list showing which one was best. Fred, the bank president, said he would lend Sam up to one thousand dollars to buy the truck. I lost one dollar and ninety cents at cards tonight, but could hardly wait until tomorrow to tell Sam the good news.

When Sam came to work on Friday morning, I told him the good news and we went to the bank to meet Fred. After Fred had explained to Sam about the terms, Fred filled out the papers and Sam signed them. He had never signed a contract before, but felt confident it was OK, because I was with him. When we were finished with the contract, Fred took us into another office to meet Joe Nichols, the auditor.

Joe was a young man, just out of college. He was very personable, well dressed, and you just knew he would be a success. He was thin, wavy hair, and deep brown eyes, and a ready smile. I am sure that is why the bank hired him in the first place. Joe's family was one of the oldest families in the city and was quite well to do. I wondered why Fred was so anxious for us to meet Joe, but dismissed it from my mind. Fred told us the auction would be the following Saturday, a week away. Sam had never been to an auction and asked me to go with him.

CHAPTER 7

KITCHEN AND BATHS

Back to the house and we finished the odds and ends and cleanup of the walls and the plaster jobs. At about 4 in the afternoon a large truck pulled up. Would you believe it was Sarah and Derrick and another helper. They had the cupboards for the kitchen, plus the sinks and toilets and everything else for the bathrooms. They had even brought the tiles for the walls and floor. They had planned to work over the weekend and install everything before they left. Before Nate, John and Sam went home, we unloaded all the material and put it in the house. I made arrangements for Nate, John and Sam to work over the weekend to help install everything. Sarah showed me pictures of the material they had brought. This was the latest design that she had made. I was amazed; she had incorporated all the latest gadgets in her design. After looking at the pictures, I called the motel and reserved three rooms. I then suggested we all go out to eat. The helper said he was tired and declined the invitation. He would grab a sandwich at the motel and turn in. Since I hadn't seen Sarah for over three years, we had a lot of catching up to do. First, she had graduated from college in three years. She knew more about design of kitchens and bathrooms than the instructors and had been offered a part time job teaching. Then came the big news that she and Derrick were getting married. They were going to announce it at Emily's wedding, but wanted me to know beforehand.

I congratulated them and told them I had expected they would get married. I asked what kind of wedding and they told me a small church wedding with only the family and a few friends attending. I said I would be there with bells on. This was the main reason they had brought the stuff down. I could have talked all night, but I knew they were tired, so I took them to the motel and I went home to bed. I had trouble imagining how everything always fell into place.

Saturday morning about 8 am and everybody showed up to start. It was agreed that John would help the helper start in the bathroom, setting up the shower stall and the sink cabinet, the counter top and the sink. Sarah had certainly picked out top of the line fixtures. Derrick was certainly a whiz on kitchens. First he located the studs in the wall and then produced a print showing the location of all the cabinets. Next was a leveling strip that he attached to the wall. In the meantime, Nate and Sam were unpacking the cabinets. We started in a corner and the top cabinets were installed about as fast as Nate and Sam were unpacking them. About 9:30 we had a slight interruption. Up drove the big shining Lincoln Town car and out stepped Miz Rose. She had heard of the arrival of the truck and Sarah and Derrick, and had come to meet them. I introduced Miz Rose and she insisted we all come to dinner Sunday night at 6:00 pm. Sarah and Derrick both liked Miz Rose and we agreed to be there.

By Sunday night all the cupboards were installed, the counter top and sink were all in place. The island was not put together yet as they wanted to tile the floor and the island would be in the way. Ida had been doing the cooking on the grill and she made sure nobody was hungry. Everybody quit early to get ready to go to Miz Rose's at 6:00.

I picked up Sarah and Derrick at the motel and we drove to Miz Rose's house. Talk about a feast, Miz Rose really outdid herself. Course after course after course and each one was more delicious than the one before. Miz Rose had a housekeeper who helped with the serving. After eating so much, we could hardly move. We had coffee and sat and talked. Miz Rose told us how her ancestors had started the tobacco plantation over two hundred years ago. There was no town then and after the civil war and the slaves were freed, her ancestors decided they could not operate the plantation without slaves, so they sold the land. One of the sons liked young slaves and fathered four or five children with the slaves. No records were kept, so no one really knew which children were his. Many of the slaves left the plantation to find work and the colored people who still lived in the town were the ancestors of the slaves and still lived in the shacks where the slaves lived. The town grew, but the colored people were discriminated against and forced to live in the rundown shacks. They were denied the chance for jobs and education. She said she never expected to sell the old plantation until I came along. And when I befriended the Lee kids and hired Nate and John, I hastened the change that many people in the town were looking for. She said she hoped the changes would continue. Sarah and Derrick were very impressed and asked Miz Rose to come to their wedding. They would send her an invitation. This has been an evening to remember.

Monday morning and everybody was on the job by 8:00 am. I looked at the window and suddenly realized that windows were all open. I rushed over to Home Depot to pick up polyethylene to cover the windows. As soon as I got back, Sam and I covered the windows. John and the helper were working on the second bathroom and Derrick was putting the tile over the counter. The tile has to set about 24 hours before the grouting can begin, so derrick went into the bathroom to do the floor. The tile has to be down and grouted before the toilet can be installed. Sarah and derrick did the layout for the tile and Derrick had shown Nate how to cut tile. By noon the bathroom floor tile was down. John and the helper were finished with the shower stall and the sink in the second bathroom, so we stopped for lunch. Ida had done a good job on the grill and we had hamburgers, macaroni salad, baked potatoes and roasted corn on the cob. With meals like this, how can a person get back to work in half an hour? We will work a little late tonight, so we can finish tomorrow. After lunch, everybody worked on the tile and the island for the kitchen. We left the island in the living room, so it does not interfere with the tile. The only thing left to do tomorrow is to grout the tile. I made arrangements with Ida to have a big picnic tomorrow afternoon. I called Miz Rose and invited her, she accepted. I then called Mrs. Sims who has been tutoring the kids and invited her. Mrs. Sims was very happy to be invited and said it would be a good chance for the kids to show off their new table manners. She had been teaching this at lunchtime, while they ate their lunch. I wanted Sarah and Derrick to meet the kids.

We set the time to begin at 2:00. We finished the grouting about 11, except for polishing the tile, which we could do tomorrow. Sarah, Derrick and the helper went to the motel to cleanup, and they arrived back just before 2:00. At exactly 2:00 Miz Rose drove up and she had brought three key lime pies and a big dish of candied yams with marshmallows. A few minutes later Mrs. Sims drove up with the kids. She made sure the kids were cleaned up and looked their best. I introduced the kids to Sarah and Derrick and they were very surprised. Mrs. Sims not only had been teaching them school work, but also, manners and how to meet people. When I introduced Bay to Sarah,

Bay said, "How do you do, mam." Even I was surprised. The other kids followed suit, and the same when they met Derrick, although he was called "Sir."

The picnic was a great success and I had a chance to talk to Mrs. Sims on the kids' progress. She said she was amazed at how much and how quickly they had learned. She seemed sure they would be ready for school in the fall. We spent the entire afternoon eating, talking and enjoying ourselves. Miz Rose's key lime pies just topped off the picnic and of course Sarah wanted the recipe. After the picnic was over and everyone had gone home, Sarah asked me how and why I had decided to buy this place.

I asked her and Derrick to walk with me down the lane to the dock, and on the way I recounted the day that Lucy's spirit had come to me and told me to buy this place, that I would be happy here. She then walked out on the dock and disappeared. Neither Sarah nor Derrick had anything to say, so we walked back to the house.

Before they left, I asked Derrick if he had a bill for everything. He told me there was no bill and there wouldn't be one. I told him I would see him at Emily's wedding. I asked what time they would have breakfast and I would meet them. They said they would leave about 3:00 am and stop for breakfast along the way. It certainly was pleasant having them here with me and working on the house.

For the next few days, we polished the tile, installed the toilets and put the island in the kitchen. I also called a window contractor to come and measure the windows and gave him a contract to install the windows.

CHAPTER 8

TRUCK AUCTION

On Saturday Sam and I went to the truck auction. There were only three bidders there and five trucks were to be sold. The one that Sam wanted to bid on came up second. Sam had never been to an auction, so I had to tell him when to bid. The trucks sold very cheap and Sam bought his truck for six hundred twenty-five dollars. The auctioneer told of an upcoming real estate auction of land being sold for taxes, so I got a list of the properties to be sold. One parcel was next to the dump and the land was worthless, except it had an old road that went down into the dump. I decided then that I would purchase that parcel just to get the road. It was listed as twenty acres.

Sam could hardly wait until he got the license and insurance for his truck. On Monday morning we were at the bank to get the loan papers signed and then to the license bureau for the license. This truck was larger, so Sam would be able to haul larger loads. Fred mentioned that perhaps Sam should get someone as a front man to be sure Sam always had stuff to haul to the dump. I asked if he had someone in mind, and he said, "Sure, why not Joe Nichols?" his auditor. "He not only could solicit business, but could also keep the books. I am sure he would be interested as here he only has a part time job." Sam was agreeable, so we went into Joe's office to talk to him. It was evident that Joe had been expecting us as he had several good ideas of where he could seek more customers.

I mentioned to Joe that Sam could not read, so he would have to handle the contracts and collections. Joe said, "I have already planned that and I will be bonded so Sam doesn't have to be concerned about that." We discussed pay and finally agreed that a partnership arrangement would be better. Since Sam would be spending much more time, he would get 70% and Joe, 30% after expenses. I told them I thought they would both be independently wealthy in ten years. Fred said he would have the bank's lawyer draw up the contract. I could see that Sam would not be working for me much longer. Sam left for the license bureau to get his license for the truck and I went back to the house.

I was thinking that I had planned the job to take me three years, but I had been here only three months and I was over 50% done. I examined the house to see what remained to be done. Some electrical work remained, some lights to be installed, hot water tank installed and the service hooked up. After looking at the bedrooms, living room and dining room, I decided to wallpaper if I could find old fashioned paper. Wall to wall rugs in the bedrooms and sanding and refinishing the floors in the dining room and living room were left to do. Also the fireplace needed a lot of attention. The woodwork would need refinishing throughout the house. All the woodwork was very plain, so this would not be much of a problem. The outside would need painting as this hadn't been done for years. Much of the woodwork had been removed when we moved the walls. I decided to concentrate on finishing the electrical work, strip the woodwork, and search for old fashioned wallpaper. I would have Nate and John for another week and Sam was a question mark. I called my friend from BOCES to see if he could come this week for an electrical inspection and hook up the service. He could make it on Thursday. I called a wallpaper store and they recommended a mail order house for the wallpaper. I phoned for a catalog. Then I made a trip to Home Depot for stripper and finish for the woodwork, and made arrangements to rent a sprayer for the finish. There were also electrical fixtures that I needed and Home Depot would deliver the hot water tank. Nate and John would finish the electrical and Sam would start on the woodwork.

By Tuesday evening the electrical was all ready for inspection and Sam had made good progress on the woodwork, but needed help to finish. I called for the sprayer for Wednesday afternoon. By Wednesday evening I finished spraying the woodwork and Nate and John had reinstalled most of it. We still had the inside doors to do, and like the woodwork, not much paint was left, so we started on them. My friend from BOCES came about 10:00 and by noon he had completed his inspection and called the power company to hook up the service. When the mail came, it included the catalog for old fashioned wallpaper. I phoned Miz Rose to help me make the selections. She wasn't busy and could come right over. It was a good thing that I called her because her selections were much better than mine, and I phoned in the order.

The power company sent someone over to hook up the service. I asked Ida to make a big picnic for Friday afternoon so we could celebrate Nate and John's leaving. I invited Nate's wife to celebrate with us. I was sorry to see them leave, as I had depended on them, but was happy to see them get better jobs. They certainly had changed since the first day they came looking for a job. They had much more confidence and had learned a lot. The electrical course helped.

Thursday night at cards was quite different. We met at the usual time and had tea and cookies. Fred had news about Joe, who had been looking for customers for the loads to the dump/ He had met the owner of the garbage collection company for the town and he wanted to sell his company including two garbage trucks which were quite old but in good condition. They hadn't discussed a price or time. Fred mentioned the owner did his banking with him and he didn't think he was very successful. I told them I was going to bid on the land next to the dump on Saturday.

On Friday we finished up the doors and the woodwork and hung the doors. We quit a little early so we could enjoy the picnic. I told both Nate and John how much I had enjoyed working with them and would miss them. I thought they were almost ready to cry. On Monday they would start their new job with my friend from BOCES.

Saturday morning I was at the courthouse for the tax auction. The auction started at 10:00 and there were a few parcels before the one I was interested in. Before the auction started, the auctioneer stated the terms. Cash or certified check and the county would issue a bill of sale. The deed for the land would be sent in the mail a few days later. Also the bidder would be liable for back taxes. When the property came up, the auctioneer said he had a bid of one hundred dollars for the property, so I bid two hundred dollars and was high bidder. I paid the auctioneer's office and was told I would have to come to the clerk's office to pay the taxes. I decided to go look at the property and examine the road to the dump. The road was passable but brush and limbs would have to be trimmed before using the road. Otherwise, the land was useless, just a big hole in the ground and steep banks all the way to the lake. But the road was well worth the price I had paid. At least I had a way to get to the stuff in the dump. I kept checking the dump every day, but no new material was ever there.

Sunday afternoon I got a call from Emily. They had set the date for the wedding. It was Friday, June 9th and "could you come a couple of days early to be fitted for a tuxedo?" "Sure" I would leave on Monday and drive to be there Monday evening or Tuesday morning. It would be a small church wedding with only a few friends and family. Dan would be there with his girlfriend from college, Sarah and Derrick, and of course, Mr. and Mrs. Childs. I made a mental note to call Mr. and Mrs. Childs by their first names, as they were practically members of the family.

On Monday morning I got a call from the window contractor. Could they start Tuesday morning? "Of course!" I asked Sam to be there Tuesday morning with his truck to get rid of the debris from the old windows. Most of the window frames needed extensive reworking to properly fit the new windows. As the new windows were installed, we put the polyethylene back on to cover the windows. I had planned to spray paint the outside and did this to keep the paint off the new windows. By Friday night the contractor and his helper had the windows installed. They really made an improvement in the appearance of the house.

Thursday night cards seemed a little different; everyone seemed tired and not interested in cards. I mentioned Bay's mother and how she had changed. She no longer drank. She showered every day and looked presentable. I suggested that if she had a job, she could get off welfare. I was asked what she could possibly do, what kind of work. I suggested dishwashing and cleanup at the school cafeteria. She would need good references to get a job there. The judge said he would speak to the people in the Welfare Department; maybe they could help. We stopped playing cards early. Nobody lost or won much.

On Monday I decided to paint the outside of the house. So I went off to Home Depot to rent a sprayer and get the latex paint. The house had originally been painted white, but there was very little paint left, but I decided to stay with the white color. I could do almost all the house with the sprayer except around the windows and doors, which would have to be done with a brush. Rather than put up the scaffold, I used the ladders and used scaffold brackets along with the planks we had used for the scaffolds. By Tuesday evening I had completed all I could do with the sprayer, so I cleaned the sprayer and returned it to Home Depot. On Wednesday I started on the trim around the windows and doors. I really needed two coats with the brush. By Thursday evening this was all done. On Thursday afternoon I received a special delivery of the wallpaper.

Thursday night at cards the judge had something to report about Bay's mother and her job at the school. The welfare department would try to help her get a job at the school. The school did not have any Negroes on their payroll, so that may be a problem. I told Miz Rose that I had received the wallpaper. She said she would come over tomorrow to check our selections to see how they fit. I had decided to teach Ida how to apply the wallpaper. When Miz Rose came over, we decided that our choices of the wallpaper were OK, so we could start.

I decided to paint the ceilings before putting on the wallpaper. The bedrooms all had wallpaper that would go well with a very light blue ceiling. It had to be a very light blue, almost white with a blue tint. I used a long handled roller and it didn't take long to do the three bedrooms. Naturally I put down tarp on the floor to catch any drips from the roller. Next we had to put sizing on the walls before the wallpaper. We also rolled this on with a roller, but had to brush the sizing next to the ceiling and the baseboard. The sizing had to dry thoroughly before putting on the paper, but by the time we did three bedrooms, the first bedroom was OK to start. It was almost quitting time, so we set up the wallpaper to start next morning.

I explained to Ida that the corners of a room are seldom plumb and that the first piece on a wall had to be plumbed so that it would look right, and to overlap the paper slightly in the corner. I had set a sheet of plywood on sawhorses for a table to cut the paper on. I showed her how to match the paper so the pattern continued around the room. The walls were eight feet high and the baseboard was eight inches and our border around the top was six inches. I figured that we would start the strip about three inches from the ceiling and allow two inches at the bottom for trimming. Each strip would be seven feet and three inches long. After matching, we had about twelve inches waste on each strip. The width of the paper was 22 inches. We measured 21 inches from the corner and used a straight edge and a level to draw the plumb line. We were now ready to begin. I had purchased prepasted paper and all the necessary tools including the pan to soak the wallpaper. I cut a piece of ½ inch pipe to put on the inside of the rolled up strip of paper to make it easier to soak the strip. We matched the pattern and cut three strips. The first wall was an outside wall and had a window after three strips. We lined up the first strip with the plumb line and smoothed the strip on to the wall and into the corner. Naturally we had soaked the strip before putting it on the wall. The first corner showed the necessity of the plumb line, the excess to the other wall varied between one half and one inch. We wiped down the first strip with a damp cloth to remove any glue.

I neglected to tell in detail how to soak the strips, so will do so now. Roll up the strip loosely, about three inches in diameter with the pattern on the inside and the glue outside. Place the pipe inside the roll and place in the container of warm water. After soaking about half a minute, taking hold of the outside end and very slowly unroll the strip to thoroughly soak the glue. Tip the strip a little sideways and most of the water will run off. Any drips would be caught by the tarp on the floor. Step up on the stepladder to start at the top, place next to the strip on the wall and match the pattern carefully, especially at eye level and bring the edges together. With the brush smooth the paper to the wall.

Should there be any bubbles use the plastic tool used for trimming and push the bubbles out the side. As you gain experience, the chance of bubbles will diminish. Now check the seam between the two strips. Make sure the pattern matches and the two strips touch. Next take the small roller and gently roll the seam. Now the third strip will be a little tricky. The window is 19 inches from the edge of the previous strip. We will cut another strip before soaking strip #3, so we can match the pattern. Since strip #3 has to be trimmed, have the scissors handy. Now put the edges together and match the pattern and brush over next to the window.

Next take the scissors and cut the paper at the top of the window, allowing at least two inches extra for trimming. Brush this portion to the wall and go to the bottom of the window and cut this again. After brushing this portion, cut out the excess again allowing extra for trimming. Brush again, making sure the part next to the window is stuck. Do not trim at this time; it is easier to trim if the paper is dry. Now to cut the pieces above and below the window. Using the cut strip, measure the amount needed and cut. I use a knife and a square to cut the paper so the ends are always straight. Now using the strip, go to the bottom and repeat the process. Both of these pieces will be small so just soak them in the water and apply as usual.

Now on the other side of the window you will need a plumb line again. From this point on, always have at least one strip cut ahead. The window is 29 inches and the trim is 10 inches, so the waste would be about 10 inches. Using the process as on the other side of the window, except line up the paper with the plumb line first. Then on to the corner strip.

One basic thing to remember, always put a plumb line after every corner, every door and every window. Now to a corner, remember you have to overlap each corner. If the corner takes less than a full sheet, you must cut the strip lengthwise. First measure the distance to the corner and add one inch to go around the corner. Cut, wet and apply the strip to the corner as usual. Make sure to brush the paper into the corner. Measure the piece left and draw your plumb line that distance from the corner. Wet this piece and apply with the edge to the plumb line. The corner will not match the pattern exactly, but will be close enough to not be noticeable.

Follow these directions until the room is finished. The bottom can be trimmed anytime after a few minutes drying time. Use the plastic straight edge to cut off the excess. Use a very sharp knife and change the blade often. Use the same method around the windows and doors. Don't forget to wash off any glue from the area after trimming. The only thing left is the border.

First match the ends of two rolls. Measure down from the ceiling the width of the border and mark about every three feet. The ceiling won't be level so these marks are only guides. When wetting the border, the piece will be 15 feet or more long, so the piece has to be folded for easy handling. Do not crease the folds. After the first piece, this will be easy. Start in a corner and allow extra for overlap. As you place the border on the wall, be sure to brush out creases. Both the ceiling and the marks are only guides. It is more important to have the full border showing than to follow the marks or the ceiling. For the second and succeeding pieces, match the ends and continue around the room. Don't forget to wipe any excess glue off the border. Follow this procedure on all the rooms.

The first bedroom took more than one day as I was very careful that Ida understood each step and why we did it this way. Ida was a good pupil and was very interested in learning. I knew when we were done that her house would be next. By Thursday night we were on the third bedroom. I had checked the fireplace and decided that I needed a good mason to repair it. When I got to Miz Rose's Thursday evening, everybody was more interested in talking than playing cards. First Miz Rose had prepared a dip with rye bread or crackers and then the crowning glory, key lime pie. The judge reported he had heard from the Welfare department and they had talked to the school. Their first impression was an emphatic "No", but after the Welfare department had told them what the law was and possibly losing jobs, they relented and said they would give Bay's mother a chance. We decided that the odds against her were about 95 to 5. We decided Miz Rose would go talk to her and explain the situation to her. I would send Ida to buy the white pants and shirts that she would need.

Next Fred wanted to talk about the deal with the garbage man. He would like to sell the business July 1. He and Joe Nichols had decided on a price that was reasonable and it was time to discuss this with Sam, his partner. I said I would talk to Sam and set up a meeting. They even recommended a mason to do the work on the chimney. We never did play cards, but I didn't care, I had half a key lime pie to take home.

Friday morning I sent Ida to get the clothing. Miz Rose said she would talk to Bay's mother over the weekend and she would go to the Welfare department on Monday. They would take her to the school.

I called the mason and his wife said he was on a job, but she would tell him to call that night. When Ida got back, we started on the living room. I really wanted to sand the floor first, but decided that could wait. We painted the ceiling first using an off white latex paint. By Saturday afternoon we were finishing the wallpaper on the walls and Miz Rose drove up. She had just finished talking to Bay's mother and had told her how important it was that she do a good job. Ida said she would take the uniforms over and give them to her after we finished work. Of course Miz Rose made an inspection of the wallpaper. I knew she would be critical, but she was pleased with the result. She mentioned that I would soon be ready for some furniture. After Miz Rose left, Ida and I finished the border, cleaned up and quit for the day.

Sunday morning I went to Sam's house to set up the meeting with Fred and Joe about buying the garbage business. Sam questioned me to see if I thought this would be a good deal for him. I assured him that I thought with Joe as his partner, it would be a terrific deal. He would have to renegotiate a new contract with Joe to give him a larger percentage of the profit. Sam said he would be available Monday morning, so I told him to meet me at the bank. I asked Sam's wife what she thought of the deal. She said she would trust my decision. I invited her to join us in the meeting on Monday morning.

Monday morning was very busy. Ida came to work early so Bay's mother could shower and get ready for her appointment. I met Sam and his wife at the bank about 9:30. We had a lot to discuss. First was the new partnership agreement. Joe would take care of the business end, collect the money, pay the bills and solicit new business and Sam would handle the trucks, the help and the scheduling for pickup. Joe made notes of all the agreement and would give them to the bank's lawyer to draw up the agreements. Since Sam had already made several payments on his truck, Fred said he would loan the money for the deal. Both Sam and his wife told me later that this was a dream come true and they could hardly wait until the deal was complete. Joe said he thought the lawyer should have all the papers completed in a week and he would call me when they were ready.

When I got back to the house, Ida was still there and talking to the mason, who was there about the chimney. He had already checked the outside and determined he could save it, but it would need a lot of work. He was ready to check the inside. The inside was quite similar to the outside. It could be saved, but would require a lot of repair. He suggested a metal insert in the chimney and a wood burning stove. He would remove all the loose mortar and patch all the cracks with concrete. I asked for a price, but he said it would be impossible to be firm on the price, but it would be about five thousand. He would not be able to tell how long it would take. I asked when he could start and he said in about a month, about June 20th. He had several small jobs to complete before this one.. We agreed upon a daily rate of pay and I gave him the OK to start.

After the mason left, I asked Ida about Bay's mother. She got ready to go and Ida had driven her to the welfare department at 9 am.

She hadn't heard anything since then. About 4 pm Miz Rose drove up to see how Bay's mother had made out. Mrs. Sims drove up shortly after with Bay, Benny and Jada. She dropped them off at their house and drove on over to join us. Everybody wanted to know the decision.

A few minutes later Bay's mother and the three kids walked over to the house. They were all smiles, so it was easy to see that she had the job and had come over to thank us. She was very happy to be off welfare, but would still have the insurance until she had insurance from the school. She thanked Miz Rose and promised her that she would work hard to keep the job. She also thanked Mrs. Sims for tutoring the kids. They spent hours every night studying and Bay would tutor the two younger kids. They would all be ready to attend school in the fall. I was very happy for Bay's mother, not only did she have a job, but she had it with a local government agency. She had broken the barrier that had existed for years. I thought Miz Rose was going to cry; she was so happy. We all congratulated Mrs. Lee and she was beaming she was so happy..

It is now only ten days before I leave for Emily's wedding. Ida was kept very busy everyday seeing that everybody got their showers, doing the washing, and driving the kids to Mrs. Sims' house. Thursday night at cards everybody had so much to talk about, we never played cards. We just sat and talked, ate cookies and drank hot tea. Everybody was happy about Bay's mother. We hoped she would do a good job and fit in with the other help. We talked about Sam and Joe's partnership and the garbage business and we all thought this would be a winner. We also talked about the Lee kids and their starting school in the fall. This also would be a first and would open the way for the other kids. Things were beginning to change. I really didn't feel like starting any new project before leaving for Emily's wedding, so I decided I would do a little shopping and get ready for the trip.

On Friday Joe called and said the lawyer had all the papers ready to sign and he asked if we could be at the bank Monday morning. I went to see Sam and found that he was available, so I called Joe and said we would be there. The meeting was quite short and all the papers were signed including the loan papers from the bank. Joe had made arrangements with the owner, so that he and Sam would spend three weeks observing the routes and all aspects of the business. Joe had also made arrangements with the owner to meet on Tuesday morning to sign the purchase papers. Sam said he would be there, so that was all settled.

On Monday evening Bay and his mother came over to the trailer. Mrs. Lee was crying, and told me what a tough time she had at work. All the employees insulted her all day and did everything possible to get her to quit. I called Miz Rose and explained the problem and she came right over. Between us, we told Mrs. Lee that was what she could expect for awhile. The best way to counteract it was to smile and not take the insults seriously. "Just do your work and keep smiling,

Hopefully it would get better." She said she would try. After Mrs. Lee and Bay left, Miz Rose and I talked about her problem and we hoped Mrs. Lee could hang in there until things got better.

On Tuesday morning Sam stopped to see if I would go to the bank with him to sign the papers for the purchase of the business. I agreed and told Sam I would meet him at the bank at 9:00 am. The meeting didn't take long, but the applications for the licenses and permits had to be taken care of. Joe would handle all this. The real estate, garage for the truck and office would be finalized on the day before Sam and Joe took over the business. Sam had planned to spend the next three weeks learning the routes and seeing how everything was handled. Joe would go into the office and get acquainted with all the office procedures, especially billing and the list of customers, and bring the employee paperwork up to date.

After the papers were signed and everything was arranged, I decided to go shopping and buy myself some new casual clothes to wear

to Emily's wedding. I had the truck serviced and everything checked for the trip. I had originally planned to leave on Sunday, but decided to leave on Friday. I would make the trip a vacation. I kept going over all the details for two days, picked up new maps and checked the route I would take.

At cards on Thursday night I couldn't get my mind on the cards and lost nine dollars and eighty cents. This was the biggest amount anyone had ever lost. We discussed the trip and Miz Rose said she was looking forward to Sarah's wedding.

After I got home I decided to walk down to the dock. I sat down on the dock and started thinking about everything that had happened in the last six months, and was surprised at how much at peace I felt. Finally I went back to the trailer and to bed. Tomorrow will be a busy day.

Not being able to sleep much, I was up at 5:00 am and was excited about seeing the kids. The packing was finished last night. The only thing left to do was breakfast and check the dump before I leave. I had the usual breakfast of coffee and cereal. There was nothing new at the dump, no activity or additions. Now to start the truck and begin the trip.

CHAPTER 9

EMILY'S WEDDING

The trip itself was about 800 miles. I could have made it in one day, but I decided to spend two days on the trip and do some sightseeing along the way. Actually nothing special happened at any of the places I stopped. I snapped a few pictures, but there was nothing to get excited about. I arrived in Buffalo about 2:00 pm and checked into the Amherst Inn. After checking in, I thought I would drive around to see the neighborhoods I used to know so well. This was not a good idea as it brought back memories of Lucy and our life together. I didn't even want to see old friends, so I went back to the motel. I called Emily to tell her I had arrived and find out where the kids were staying. She gave me the details of the wedding. The wedding would be at the Unitarian Church on Elmwood Avenue and dinner would be at the Roycroft Inn in East Aurora. I was familiar with the church as Lucy and I had gone there. The wedding would be on Tuesday at 11:00 am. I was very familiar with the Roycroft Inn as it had been remodeled by Vince who was a friend of mine. We had eaten there often. Neither affair was to be large, only family and a few friends. Both Dan and Sarah and the

Childs were staying at the Roycroft. I was sorry I had not thought to stay there myself.

Emily asked if I would be available for a tux fitting on Monday morning and I said, "Sure". She then invited me to join them all at the Roycroft Inn for dinner. Vince was famous for his prime rib and I had my special end cut. Talk about good eating, this was "fit for a king". The dinner was really special and conversation terrific; the only problem was calling the Childs by their first names, Bernard and Wanda. Sarah was her usual lively self, joking and laughing. What an evening, and what a wonderful family. I hadn't enjoyed myself so much in years.

We all agreed to meet at the Unitarian Church for services at 10:00 am Sunday. One thing I had forgotten to mention: I was very impressed with Tom Watson, Emily's choice for a husband and Dan's girlfriend, Judy who was also in med school. They had all made good choices and had my blessing.

After such a wonderful evening, I really didn't relish going back to the motel, but went anyway and got ready for bed. As usual I was up at 6:00 am, got dressed and had breakfast. There would probably be many old friends at the church, but I was surprised to see only one couple that I knew. What a difference three years makes!

Our group arrived by 10:00 and everybody was happy. The Unitarian Church is beautiful, no ceiling, but huge beams overhead and all stained natural. This was the first time I had been to church for over three years and I was really impressed with the service.

We decided on an early lunch and then Emily and Tom would show us their new home. We spent over two hours at lunch and then went off to see the house. The house was only a couple of years old and very nice. Of course Sarah and Derrick and Bernard and Wanda headed for the kitchen and bathrooms. Sarah immediately offered to do the remodeling and install all her latest ideas. Emily politely refused and said she would have to do with a two year kitchen and bathrooms. Emily had already purchased some of their furniture, so they were well on their way.

We decided to go to the Roycroft again for dinner, as we were nearby. As usual, the meal was fantastic and we all enjoyed it. Emily reminded me to be at the tux fitting at 9:00, and that was not a problem. All of this socializing was more than I was used to, so I decided to call it a day and go back to the motel. I was a little tired and decided to take off my shoes and lie across the bed. I woke up about 11:00 and decided it was time to go to bed.

I was up at the usual time, had breakfast, and dressed to go to the fitting.

Sarah and Dan came with Emily and we met at the tux rental place. The fitting didn't take long, only minor adjustments, and it would be ready by 4:00. Emily had some last minute errands to do, so Sarah, Dan and I decided to go past our house. It hadn't changed much. There were several children playing in the yard. Suddenly, out of the blue, Sarah said, "Dad, I want to ask you a question. When are you and Miz Rose getting married?" I was completely shocked. We had never even discussed marriage, and I told Sarah so. She said, "You would be happy together." I promised to talk it over with Miz Rose when I got back.

Sarah was going to announce her wedding at the reception and Dan said that he and Judy were discussing marriage, but hadn't set a date. I thought I was spending an afternoon with my kids, but realized they were now adults.

It was getting close to 4:00, so we decided to pick up the tux and go to the motel for a snack. The snack turned out to be a lovely meal. I had never realized till now how much I missed the kids. We ate and talked until well after 8:00 and then I decided it was time to take them to the Roycroft. Tomorrow is the big day. We had gone over the plans several times, so we all knew what to do.

Tuesday, June 9th was a beautiful day with sun shining, hardly a cloud in the sky. Emily looked beautiful in her wedding gown; Lucy would have been so proud. The wedding went without a hitch and I was so proud walking down with aisle with Emily.

The reception started at 4:00 at the Roycroft with drinks, but with a group that doesn't drink much, the snacks disappeared before the drinks. I had promised to pay for the reception, so I told Vince that I wanted the best and plenty of it. Vince didn't disappoint me. Everything was perfect. After we finished eating, Sarah and Derrick stood up and announced their wedding date, September 3rd, which happened to be Wanda Childs' birthday. Of course, we were all invited. Next came Dan and Judy; they announced their wedding but no date had been set. It was obvious the date was not far away. The evening was perfect and everyone had a wonderful time. Emily and Tom were leaving tomorrow morning for a cruise, so we ended the celebration early.

CHAPTER 10

BACK HOME

I wanted to make the trip back in one day; I was anxious to talk to Miz Rose and check to see how my trap in the dump was working. I woke up about 4:00 am and decided to get an early start, so I got up, got dressed and started on my way, figuring to stop for breakfast somewhere on the way. There was a little restaurant in southern Pennsylvania where I stopped. I didn't want much as I had eaten so much in the last three days that I wasn't hungry. However, I had a waffle and coffee and bought a sandwich for on the way. I gassed up and was on my way. The total stop time was 42 minutes. In the middle of the afternoon I stopped at a rest area and ate the sandwich along with a Pepsi to wash it down. I was making good time, 600 miles in a little over twelve hours with only 200 miles to go. It was well after dark when I pulled off the intrastate highway. The lights were on in the dump and I could see my trap had worked. More old tires and even a couple of refrigerators or freezers were there. Now if the cameras had done their job, I was in business. I would call the camera man tomorrow to check the film.

When I called the camera man, he was as excited as I was to see what was on the tape. He said he would check it right away. By noon he had the results. The cameras had done their job. The town and the local tire company had both been caught dumping along with the local appliance store. Their trucks and license plates were all visible on the tapes. Since this was Thursday and gin night, I took the tapes along. I wanted to ask the judge, who was the proper lawyer to handle the case. The judge said he had the perfect person for the job and he seldom lost a case. He lived in the next town and he gave me his name and telephone number. With all this excitement I wasn't able to talk with Miz Rose. Another time!

Early Friday morning I called the lawyer and told him the judge had recommended him for the job. He asked if I was free this afternoon to show him the film. After viewing the film, he said this case was right up his alley. What did I want to get out of the job? #1: They pay for cleaning up the dump. #2: The town would furnish a loader to load the stuff. #3: Pay the lawyer's fee. I explained that I had bought the property next door, which had a road to the dump. The lawyer thought this was a good deal for him and said he would start Monday morning.

I thought that I had better check with Sam and his partner Joe to see how they were doing. Joe had found out that the customers biggest complaint was the noise that the garbage handlers were making, so he was changing the rules. Instead of the garbage man going back to get the garbage and the customer furnishing the garbage cans, the company would furnish plastic garbage cans on wheels and the customer would bring the container to the street. The only extra charge was 25 cents a week. Sam liked this idea, as it would save over one hour per day per truck and eliminate the noise. Sam and Joe were good partners; they thought a lot alike. Several of the garbage handlers had already quit. They didn't like a black boss. No matter, they were replaced by young black men. I asked Sam if he could manage cleaning up the dump, and he said "Yes, I already have a part time driver for the truck." Joe and Sam were on the road to being successful. Joe had been so busy that he really hadn't been out looking for new business. That would come later. I mentioned to Joe about Sam cleaning up the dump, and wanted Sam to make enough profit to pay for his truck. Joe liked the idea.

The lawyer called right after lunch. He had met with the owners of the two businesses and the mayor. They had come to terms. After seeing the film, all three decided they could not win the case, so the lawyer specified the terms. The mayor would furnish the loader and a man to run it as their share. The other two would pay all the dumping fees and the hauling costs. I don't know how much the lawyer charged, but I am sure he didn't short change himself. I called Sam and told him to get someone to clear the roadway. Sam had the garbage handlers work a few hours on the roadway and it was all clear and ready to use. I would certainly have news to report at the gin game this week.

Thursday night came and I thought I had the big news, but mine was only mediocre. Mrs. Lee was doing fine; after the initial onslaught of harassment, Mrs. Lee was being accepted. Mrs. Sims had tested the Lee kids and she reported that Bay was doing fourth grade work, Benny third grade and Jada second grade. We would have to make sure the children were tested, so they would be in the proper grade. The mason would be ready to start on the chimney next week. Then the judge asked if I had heard the news about the interstate. They were going to improve it. It would be a big job taking several years. Both Sam and Joe were quite happy the way things were going. They hadn't finalized the sale yet and had solved one of the customer's biggest problems, the noise. Everyone was happy over this and they were gaining time for new customers. Joe had ordered the new container and the first shipment would be made the day the sale was final. It was only eight more days before the sale is completed. They not only had changed the rules, but also a lot of help. Even the customers could see the difference. Sam was a good boss; he told the help what he wanted and then he followed through to see that it was done his way, and quietly was one of Sam's objectives.

While Joe and Sam were getting ready to take over the business, the clean-up of the dump was to begin and another factor was coming up. It was the start of the hurricane season. Storms were all around us and any day we could expect a storm. The hurricane came with very little warning and as usual, all the colored people came to the cave to ride out the storm. They brought food and blankets, cots and even two portable toilets. They had very specific rules in the cave. There would no booze and everyone had to cooperate to make things easy. Everything was fine except three local yokels crashed the party with enough booze to last a week. The first I knew of this was when Nate and John, my first two employees, came to ask how to handle the situation. They had never had this happen before. All the white people stayed at the school or town hall, where they were fed and furnished cots. I asked if they were drunk and the answer was "Yes". I told them to get all the men and confront the yokels and tell them they could stay, but they had to follow the rules. No booze! They could destroy the booze or leave. And if they refused, break every bottle and forcibly put them out, but no one was to get hurt. Be sure of that.

Nate and John left and later I heard how it was handled. Each man got a club or whatever was handy and they all confronted the yokels. The yokels decided it was time to go, so they left. The booze was destroyed.

The next day I went over to see how they were doing, and told Nate and John to get the generator so they could have lights.

That week at cards I told Miz Rose that I needed furniture. I wanted some of the original furniture in the old plantation. She informed me that the slaves probably received some of the furniture and I should inquire there first. She had a couple of bedroom sets that she would give me. I passed the word around that I was looking for the original furniture. I received some beautiful pieces and a lot of pieces that needed repairs. I sent the things that needed repair to a local antique dealer who did a good job cleaning and repairing. When I got through, the place looked like a museum. Of course, it took over one year to get all the furniture in place.

Now it was time to get back to the job of cleaning the dump. First, there were all the old tires, water, mosquitoes, snakes and bugs. Every night they would spray for mosquitoes and every day there were a million more. After two weeks with two loads each day, it was cleaned up. The State inspector gave us a clean slate. The good thing was it didn't cost me anything and Sam got his truck paid for.

In the meantime the Lee kids were registered for school. Miz Rose and Mrs. Sims went with the children to register. The superintendent wanted to put them all in first grade and the judge had to tell the superintendent what the law was. If he valued his job, he would test the kids. End of story!

The kids were tested with Bay in 4th grade, Benny in 3rd grade and Jada in second. When the Lee kids were registered, seven more colored kids were registered in first grade. Things were changing. The area where the colored people lived also was changing. Now that some of them had jobs, they were fixing up their houses. Ida was teaching other women how to paper a room and some of the houses were painted. John and Nate were kept busy repairing and roofing houses, but no electricity yet.

Sam and Joe were doing well. They were busier and had a lot of new customers. Best of all, the customers were happy with the service.

June and July came and went and we started to think about Sarah's wedding. At Miz Rose's on Thursday night I told Miz Rose that I would rent a car for our trip to Sarah's wedding. The judge mentioned that the state was looking for a place to dump excess fill. He asked if I would be interested. "How much do they have?" "A lot, probably fill for the entire dump." "If you are interested, go see the person in charge and he can tell you the details." "I'll see him next week." "Better make it tomorrow. A lot of people are looking for this contract." "I will plan to go first thing tomorrow."

Miz Rose asked if we wanted Mrs. Sims to continue teaching the Lee kids and we all agreed; give them as much advantage as we can.

Friday morning I was at the interstate job site. The first question the man asked was how big the hole to be filled in was and how much would I charge per load. I pointed to a couple of large hills and said he could probably put both hills in the hole. I was more interested in the finished product than the compensation. I wanted it to be a park for the town with grass and trees and a couple of tennis courts and a softball diamond. He became interested right away and asked when he could see it. I said, "Right now." So he called over a couple of surveyors to check the property. When he saw the property, the surveyor didn't even take down their transit. He said it was just what they were looking for and he would send someone on Monday to draw up the contract. I called the lawyer who worked on the dump and asked him to represent me. The lawyer said he would see me on Saturday to discuss details.

When he arrived on Saturday morning, he had on his work clothes and boots along with a camera, and we looked at the whole property. I told him what I expected, a finished park with trees, roads, lights, drinking fountains, tennis courts, softball diamond and a chain link fence around everything. The lawyer said, "I think you are forgetting something. How about a swimming beach?" "Where?" "In what is now the mud puddle at the end of the lake. You can bring in the sand from the sand bar about 50 yards in the lake and have a nice sandy beach. We will charge the State a small dumping fee to pay for moving the sand." No wonder the judge liked this lawyer; he was "on the ball." He had taken a lot of pictures that dictate the size of the park. It would be almost 40 acres.

Most of Monday was taken up with the contract, but when we finished, everything was covered, including a sign that said "Future Home of Lucy's Park". Although dumping could begin right away, trees had to be cut down and the fence put up. The fee was set at one dollar per load to be paid monthly and the State would monitor how many loads. There was even a provision for repairing the road and the paved area overlooking the dump. I had retained the road to the dock and approximately twenty feet to the side of the road and the dock. This was where the fence would go. This area was wooded and was a natural boundary. Naturally the cave was not included in the park. I thought it was time to name the roadway to the dock, so I had the lawyer draw up the papers to submit to the board to call it "Lucy's Way" and put up the signs. At the next meeting of the board it was passed and the signs went up. The boss of the interstate project was in a hurry to start dumping, so he had a crew putting up the fence and another cutting down the trees. Dumping the first month was slow, with only about 100 loads, but the size of the loads was huge. He brought in a bulldozer to spread the fill, so he could keep dumping from the top. After the first month, the dumping increased. The fence was up and the trees down. Sometimes there would be 3 or 4 trucks in line at one time to dump. It seems as if everything is happening at the same time; Sarah's wedding, school starting, election time.

Now that many of the colored people were working, they all wanted electricity, sewer and water. They had formed a committee to see what could be done. A lot of them had never voted, so they hadn't registered. Sam had convinced Joe to run for the board and they all pledged to vote for Joe. Since Mrs. Lee was working, she had been buying the kids new school clothes, and they were all ready to start school. Ida asked if some of the neighbor's kids could shower. I told her that she was in charge and she could do what she wanted.

CHAPTER 11

SARAH'S WEDDING

In the meantime Miz Rose had received her invitation to Sarah's wedding and had bought her a set of "Southern Living" cookbooks as a wedding present. I knew what the dessert would be at Sarah's wedding, Key lime pie, baked by Miz Rose. We planned to leave four days before the wedding. Miz Rose would stay at the Childs' house, so she could make the pies. I would stay at a motel nearby. I rented a big Lincoln for the trip. I had bought a tux, so I wouldn't have to worry about a fitting. All the family would stay at the same motel. Sarah's wedding was just the opposite of Emily's wedding, big flashy, a lot of guests and news reporters and cameramen. Sarah made news wherever she went.

We arrived two days before the wedding, so Miz Rose would have time to bake the pies. It was nice seeing the kids again. Emily was back from her honeymoon and she and Tom were settling down to married life. They weren't planning children for a few years. Dan and Judy were considering just getting married by a Justice of the Peace with no frills, no time and no bother. They were too busy to take the time to be married with honeymoon and all.

Miz Rose had picked up some of the ingredients for the pies before we started just to be sure.

Wanda wanted to be sure she knew every step in the process, so she was going to help. I am sure Sarah would be there if she had the time. Even Emily and Judy got in on the pie making. They ended up with 31 pies and I am sure none went to waste.

We practiced the entire wedding ceremony the day before, so there would be no mistakes. And now came the big day. I was so proud walking down the aisle with Sarah. I could feel Lucy crying. Sarah looked beautiful in her gown and flashbulbs were going off all around us. The dinner was just as spectacular. The huge wedding cake graced the head table. Miz Rose's pies were on a separate table. Flash bulbs kept flashing the entire time. After the meal, Bernard Childs gave a short speech about welcoming Sarah to the family and mentioning how much she meant to the business. It was evident that he was very proud of her.

Miz Rose's pies were a great hit and many women wanted the recipe. While we were eating, I made Dan and Judy promise that when they got married, they would let the family know, so we could attend. I bet myself that within six months they would be married. Sarah and Derrick would be leaving the next day for Las Vegas to a builders' convention where Sarah was to give a talk on her newest designs for kitchens. That was Sarah, always mixing business with pleasure.

On the way back Miz Rose was quiet much of the trip. Finally she could contain herself no longer. She said that Sarah had embarrassed her while they were making the pies. Out of the blue she asked, "When are you going to marry my father?"

" Everybody stopped to listen for my answer and I said, 'He has never asked me.'"

And so I turned to her and said, "Well, I will ask you now. Will you marry me?"

"No, you are still involved too much with your first wife. Ask me again in about a year and I will probably say 'yes'." The rest of the trip was quiet, with not much conversation, but a lot of thinking. I finally asked her if she would go with me to Dan's wedding. And she said, "Yes."

CHAPTER 12

SCHOOL HAS STARTED

By the time we got back, school had started and it was obvious that Bay was way ahead of his class. He continued to tutor Benny and Jada, so they could excel. But Bay had a knack for learning and he continued to excel. His grades were the highest in the class. Bay was beginning to be known as the brain in the class and he wanted to maintain that reputation. Mrs. Lee was a changed woman. Now that she had a job, was off welfare, cleaned up with decent clothes, she had a boyfriend. She was seeing one of Sam's truck drivers.

Joe and Sam were doing well and the business was thriving. Joe was getting to be known as a very astute business man. But in the political arena Joe had some misgivings. His adversary had been in office a long time and was using dirty tricks to win the election. Joe had promised the colored people he would work for them to get sewer, water, and electricity. Election rhetoric got nasty and Joe's opponent figured he would use the old tactics against the blacks to win the election. But now the people saw the colored people in a different light. They could see the difference. They had jobs and many were fixing up their homes and voting. They were working to be good citizens. The old times were in the past.

Joe won the election easily, and now came the hard part, how to pay for the improvements. Sewer and water were the hard parts because major changes had to be made in existing basic proponents. In the water department the treatment plant had to be expanded and in the sewer department again, the treatment plant had to be expanded. Joe hadn't realized how many people were with him on this project, but when the issue came up for a vote, the people voted for the town to go into debt for the project.

So plans were made to increase both plants to take care of the new customers. The electric company agreed to put in the new lines if 95% of the customers agreed to sign up for the new service. The sign up rate was close to 98%. Nate and John ran a basic special to wire a house. The inspections were made by my man at BOCES, so soon everyone had electricity. Sewer and water were a little slower. The sewer treatment plant had to be expanded and the water treatment had to be upgraded. Even though all systems were go, it would be at least two years before everyone was hooked up. But they knew it was coming, so they could plan their water systems and their new bathrooms. The outhouses would soon be a thing of the past.

Funny how time flies when you are busy. Money kept piling up in the fill account and I still hadn't found anyone to move the sand bar to the beach area. I finally decided to buy the necessary equipment. I also found out why so few people were in the business of moving sand. Sand is very corrosive and the pipes or the pump don't last very long. And so I doubled my effort to find someone. Finally I found someone who had a little different system. Their pump only pumped water to carry the sand and the sand was put into the pipe with a machine that could regulate the amount of sand. This system did away with the excessive wear and was more reasonable, but they couldn't start until spring. Since the completion of the park was years away, there was no rush to start.

Every day the dumping continued on the park, but that was no longer exciting. The excitement was elsewhere. Mrs. Lee was engaged to the truck driver and the marriage was soon. Mrs. Sims, who taught the Lee kids, opened a first grade tutoring class to help the colored kids in the first grade, since their parents couldn't help. The Lee kids were doing well in school. Bay was still helping Benny and Jada and Bay was still considered the brain in his class.

Dan and Judy called to say they were graduating from med school the latter part of January and would like to get married before they started their internship in February. Could we all attend the wedding? I called Emily and Sarah and they both said they would be there. I then phoned Miz Rose, who said she could make it.

Mrs. Lee planned a small wedding with just a few close friends attending. But the colored people planned differently. They planned a big picnic after the wedding. Half of the school teachers and students came, as well as all the colored people. They really had a celebration. The judge hired a caterer to cook hot dogs, hamburgers and sausages on the grill and the colored people brought baked beans, greens, candied yams and fried chicken. The caterer set up tables to hold all the food. Last but not least was Tootle, John's younger brother. He was called Tootle because from the age of four, he was always making believe he was playing a horn. By the time he was twelve, he had a saxophone and when he was eighteen, he headed to New Orleans to play jazz. He was now twenty-five and was home for a visit. He had brought a couple of friends with him and he invited another friend to join the party.

They all brought their instruments to the party, two saxophones, a trumpet, and a clarinet. They had planned to play a few numbers to liven up the party. They played a couple of numbers, New Orleans jazz, and the crowd was so enthusiastic they kept playing. As the crowd grew more enthusiastic, the musicians got hotter. Soon the music rivaled New Orleans jazz and students were dancing everywhere. Even the staid teachers joined the fun. Tonight the "Caroline Jazz Music Ensemble" was born!!

The town had never seen such a celebration and the teachers had a new appreciation for the colored people. The celebration didn't end until after one A. M.

I would rent the big Lincoln to go to Dan and Judy's wedding, but we all planned to be there just two days. We all planned to stay in the same motel and make that our headquarters. Nothing was planned except to visit. The wedding was very small with just our group attending.

Before the ceremony, Sarah made a suggestion. Why not have a double wedding with Dan and Judy, and me and Miz Rose. Miz Rose turned thumbs down on this idea. She said that all her friends would expect a big wedding. Sarah then suggested, "How about a date?" Miz Rose had no answer for this. On the trip back home, I tried to get Miz Rose to set a date, but her remark was "The year isn't up yet." That is the only response I could get.

The Lee kids were excelling in school. When the school year ended, Bay was way ahead of his class and he was promoted to sixth grade. Benny and Jada were also promoted. I guess the teachers thought that by Bay skipping fifth grade it would slow him down a bit, but it only made him more determined to succeed. He worked harder than ever to be the brain in his class and was constantly helping others to excel.

Mrs. Sims was also coming up. She applied for and received a license to teach adult education classes, to teach adults how to read and write. Needless to say, her classes were a huge success. Many of the colored parents were her first students.

Spring comes early in the south. By the middle of February the sand people were ready to start. They set up their equipment and started pumping the sand and water into the mud. Within a few days we had an idea how it was working. The finished product would be fine; we just had to keep pumping sand for the next few months. I decided to call it "Miz Rose's Beach". It had a name even before it was a beach and before there was a road or even a path to it. When the park was completed, there would be a road and parking lot. By the end of the summer the sand would probably all be in place. I just hope we don't run out of sand.

The Town was making progress with the water and sewer systems, but hadn't started the lines yet. Although they did have specs so the people could have their piping done and the space for the bathroom completed. Nate and John had to hire extra help to keep up with the work. Joe was happy that the people were getting sewer and water. Now the interstate had expanded, new developments were being added to the town, and with the additions to the sewer and water helped. Sam and Joe's business was also growing. They were considering adding a new truck. There was even talk of a new shopping mall near the exit of the interstate. The school board was talking of adding to the existing school building, building a gym and football field with bleachers so the students could watch the game.

Bay was still shining as the brain in his class, but Benny still needed help. But what he lacked in mental capacity, he made up for in brute force. When the football team was organized, he went out for Junior varsity. The coach wished he was older, so he could play on the varsity squad. He did play on the varsity squad for four years, and in his senior year, they played the championship team and were beaten by only one touchdown.

Bay, however, continued to be the brain in his class. While in the eighth grade, he was taking two classes as a freshman in high school. His goal was to graduate high school in three years and still be valedictorian. The day Bay graduated from eighth grade, I thought about how far he had come in less than the five years.

I invited Bay and his mother to dinner, along with the judge, Miz Rose and Mrs. Sims. During dinner, the judge asked what Bay planned to take in college and what he planned do after college. To our amazement, he replied, "Political Science." He planned to be a politician. The judge told him if he was interested, he could get him a job as a page in the State Senate during the summer. Both Mrs. Lee and Mrs. Sims were so proud. Miz Rose was proud too, but she didn't say so. I guess we were all proud.

I had the dinner in my remodeled house. Everything was finished and I had a lot of the original furniture. The place looked like a museum. I told everyone that I would leave the place to the town for a museum.

The park was progressing very nicely. Four years of dumping huge loads of fill can fill up a huge hole. And the sand at the beach, each time we had a storm, a new supply of sand washed up on the sand bar. We had a huge beach and the sand extended way out into the water. The part next to the street was all filled in and tennis courts were finished as well as the softball diamond. The toilets were in and the drinking fountains were in. Even the parking area was in for the diamond and the courts. The road was in for the trucks to use, but they still had to put more fill in toward the lake. When it is completed, it will be one of the nicest parks in the state. Most do not have a beach area. When it is completed, I will turn it over to the town to maintain. The beach area is all complete, but there is no access road yet and no parking. It will probably be next year before this is completed.

The colored people had formed a committee to lease or buy the cave. They wanted to put in electricity, water and sewer when the town did the rest of the area. I sold them the cave for one dollar, if they would do the rest. I didn't feel that the cave ever belonged to me.

Within a year they had toilets, showers, refrigerator and a kitchen area, and the opening was closed off, all with volunteer labor. When the sewer and water were extended to the cave, they also ran the lines to the district and all the colored people had their water and sewer hooked up.

Joe had a big celebration, bands playing, speeches, and even the judge gave a speech. The colored people had finally joined the town.

With all the exciting things going on, we had one thing happen that was very distressing. Fred, the bank president, and our fourth at Miz Rose's on Thursday night, passed away. He had been in poor health for several months and passed away in his sleep. We really missed him in our Thursday night get-togethers. He didn't live long enough to see the result of our projects. He was buried next to his wife who died a couple of years previously.

Since Mrs. Lee had married the truck driver, they had added the bathroom and electricity. The sewer didn't run down their street and they had to install a septic tank. By the time Bay was a junior in high school, the judge got him a job locally in a senator's office. The same senator would have Bay as a page when he was in college. Bay was still planning three years in high school, and he was on schedule.

Every year Miz Rose and I would have tea together at my place on Labor Day and on December 20th. These were special days, which we planned every year. On Labor Day I would ask Miz Rose to marry me and every year she had the same excuse. December 20th was the day we first met and I gave her the letters I had found in the attic. Of course, the gin games continued on Thursday night. The park was completed the year Bay was a senior in high school. The road was completed to the beach area and the parking lot paved. The only thing left was planting trees and putting out picnic tables. The state had done a wonderful job and I was very proud.

Bay graduated from high school that year. He realized his ambition and graduated in three years. He was still considered the brain and was valedictorian of his class. He gave a wonderful speech to the class. We didn't see much of Bay for the next four years. He was busy at college; he had a full scholarship. In the summer he had his job in the senator's office. But his work ethic never changed. He was always the head of his class, had the highest grade and graduated with honors. The judge, Miz Rose and I went to his college graduation. Fred couldn't go; he had been ill and was too sick.

On a nice June morning after the graduation Bay came home. When I woke up, he was sitting at the picnic table on my porch waiting for breakfast. I took the cereal, milk and two bowls out to join him. He had come home to run for mayor. Everyone remembered Bay, so he had no trouble winning the election. He was a good mayor, expected everyone to do a full day's work and he fired them if they didn't. Since he had good connections in Washington, he was always able to get grants and money when he needed it.

When Bay was elected mayor, one of his first appointments was to select Benny as highway superintendent. This was a good choice; Benny was a no nonsense guy and he also expected people to work. Within a short time the people who wanted to loaf, no longer worked for the town. Bay had moved into his mother's old house after ten years as mayor. Bay decided he would have a big party to celebrate his ten years as mayor. He invited many of his friends from Washington, including the Senator. Of course, Miz Rose, the Judge and I were invited.

But were we surprised; talk about a political bombshell! The senator was retiring and he wanted Bay to run for his seat. With the senator's endorsement, the party would be behind him and his chances for the election were good. Of course, the whole meeting tonight was only a preview and nobody was supposed to know anything about Bay running for the Senate; the announcement would come later. We would need something large to announce the candidacy. Miz Rose finally came up with an idea. Why not dedicate the park? I had never officially turned the park over to the town, although the town did maintain it. I would call the lawyer tomorrow and make the arrangements. I also called Bay the next day and told him my plan. When did he want to announce his candidacy? At least a year in advance, but the dedication should be in the summer, so we could make it over a year. Why not July 4th, everybody's holiday? I was surprised, nobody ever mentioned the senator retiring, no newscast, not even a mention in the newspaper. It was as though it never happened.

When the time came, the lawyer drew up the papers to make it legal and Bay ordered the plaque for the dedication. There was no mention of Bay running for the Senate. This was to be a surprise at the dedication. First, the park was billed as the finest in the state. It had everything, even a swimming beach with a beautiful sandy beach and life guards. There were also picnic areas and tennis courts and a softball diamond and toilets, water fountains, shade trees, everything. All sorts of dignitaries were invited, even the Governor. First Bay was to give the dedication speech, extolling the park as the finest in the state. The senator was to give a speech announcing his retirement and then introducing Bay and his endorsement. Next came the Governor and Bay again. The ceremony was to start at 2:00 pm. Even the judge was to give a speech.

And then came the hard part. Running the election campaign. The senator had always used the same people to handle his campaign, so these people were available to Bay. Bay had helped in the previous campaign, so he knew these people and they all agreed to help Bay. One thing Bay changed. He got hold of Tootle and his gang to play Dixieland jazz.

I wouldn't say this won the election, but it might have helped. Miz Rose and I and the judge went to several of the meetings and we always thought Bay won the discussions.

The election was a hard fought affair. Always an issue was the idea of a colored senator and its effect on the white population. How could a colored person know what was good for North Carolina? Bay always tried to stay above this issue and used to tell young people to register to vote. The turnout on voting day was the heaviest in history. The election was close, but Bay won.

On election day he reserved the hotel in the capitol for election night and the acceptance speech. The colored vote won him the election.

We had canceled the Thursday night get-togethers during the campaign and after the election, we decided to start again. On the first night, we were having hot tea and key lime pie. When we were seated and before the conversation started, the judge remarked, "I got a call from the Governor today; he wanted to know who we wanted to appoint as Mayor in Bay's place.

So I told him, "Joe Nichols. He is already on the board, everyone likes him and he spearheaded the expansion of the water and sewer districts. And he is smart. I hope you both agree with my choice."

Miz Rose and I spoke simultaneously, "We agree! Joe would be our top choice." We sat around the table and talked and reminisced. Nobody felt like playing gin. The judge told about Bay's mother's boyfriend and about the no work, no eat deal and he had the same twinkle in his eye.

And Miz Rose told about the letters I had given her. We all talked about the past twenty-two years that I had been here and everything that had transpired, and how we all had cooperated for the good of the town. We all agreed that it was too bad that Fred couldn't be here to share the glory.

We had built the park with the tennis courts, softball diamond, swimming beach and all the other fine things. And the museum in my house. We had integrated the town and given the colored people the rights that they deserved.

They had decent housing, sewers, running water and the right to vote and most of all the respect of the community.

Since Miz Rose had baked only one pie, there was only one quarter of a pie for me to take home. Before I left, I told them that I dreamed last night that Lucy would be at the dock on Sunday morning to take me home. My work was finished here. Both Miz Rose and the judge disagreed.

They thought we should all grow old together, have our kids and grandkids come to visit and enjoy what we had built, all the changes we had built in the town. This did sound nice.

Sarah and Derrick now had two daughters. Emily and Tom had a boy who was eight and a girl of five. Dan and Judy had a boy who was six and Judy was pregnant again. They all planned to spend their vacation every year visiting me and enjoying the park. Sometimes they would all come at once and then we would have a grand time. Of course, Miz Rose and the judge were always included in the festivities.

CHAPTER 13

AT THE DOCK

Sunday morning in late November is beautiful in North Carolina. The sun was shining and I had breakfast on the porch, cereal and coffee. About 8:30 I decided to go to the dock to see if Lucy was there. I walked slowly down Lucy's Way until I came to the dock. There on the end sat Lucy's spirit exactly as I remembered her. I could hardly wait to hold her in my arms.

As I ran onto the dock, the whole thing collapsed and broke apart. As I sank under the waves, I could feel Lucy's arms around me and her warm body next to mine.

At about ten o'clock Miz Rose remembered Gee telling about the dream that Lucy was going to meet him at the dock and she got in her car and rushed over to Gee's place. When gee wasn't there, she went to Bay's house. Bay was having coffee with his wife and the three of them drove to the dock. When they saw the dock had collapsed, they feared the worst. They could not see a body, but the dock was so entangled that the body could easily be hidden. So they decided to call the sheriff.

The sheriff came right away with two of his deputies. In the meantime, Bay called Nate and John. Within a few minutes a crowd had collected at the dock. It didn't take long to recover the body. It was under some of the old timbers.

The autopsy showed when the dock collapsed, Gee's head had struck one of the beams and fatally fractured his skull. Miz Rose went home and called Sarah to tell her the bad news

Sarah said she would call Dan and Emily. Bay called the Governor who ordered all flags in the state to fly at half mast. Then started the controversy about the funeral.

The colored people wanted to erect a mausoleum to house the casket where the trailer used to sit. And they wanted to pay for it. But the town also wanted to contribute, but the Governor had the last say. He ruled the State could also contribute. The man from BOCES would draw the plans, Nate and John would build it. It would be stone, large enough for three caskets, Gee's, Miz Rose and the judge. Gee's body would be held in cold storage while the mausoleum was built, and it was specified not to exceed thirty days.

By Monday noon the plans were delivered to Nate and John. By 4:00 the forms for the foundation were completed and by 8:00 PM the concrete for the foundation was poured. They used special fast setting concrete to eliminate curing time. In ten days the mausoleum was built and ready for the funeral.

CHAPTER 14

THE FUNERAL

The funeral was on Friday. No school on that day so the students could attend the funeral, also the teachers. The funeral was held in the largest church in the city and it was only half big enough. Bay had called Tootle and his band, "The Caroline Jazz Ensemble", to play.

At the church they played "Swing Low Sweet Chariot", and on the way to the mausoleum they played "When the Saints Come Marching In". They walked behind the hearse carrying the body and most of the people walked with them even though it was one half mile. They played the entire way and even during the internment, although they did mute it a bit during the internment.

Bernard and Wanda had chartered a plane to bring the family down for the funeral. They had stayed at the hotel. But Miz Rose had them over for tea before they left.

Sarah got Miz Rose alone before they left and said, "Miz

Rose, I love you and I will always think of you as my mother-in-law."

Miz Rose replied, "Well, thank you. I love you too. But today I am thankful I never married your father, because now your father and Lucy can spend eternity together."

About the Author

Born July 4, 1917 in south eastern Ohio. I lived on a small farm. Father was an invalid. Drove a team on the farm from the age of eleven or twelve. Attended Ohio University and Ohio State. No degree. Majored in production management. Came to New York State in 1940. Married twice. First time 22 year, second 40 years. Four daughters, one deceased. Second wife died May 2008. Previous book, *George's Tale of Yesteryear*, which is autobiographic and was written for my family. The next book is a novel and deals with integration in North Carolina in the late 1960's.